What others are saying

Travel with Jack Parker's lead character, Jeff Thornton, to the Patagonian region of Argentina. Become engulfed in the country, the vivid description of its geography, culture and fauna. A spectral confrontation, thievery and life threatening situation add to the excitement and possessiveness of the story. For those who enjoy tales of travel and mystery, this is a great read.

Robert Fetz MD, Urologist (retired)

Parker does an excellent job of enticing the reader of *Patagonian Adventure*, the second book in his series, to want to read the next chapter. The plot is well developed, and one exciting movement leads to the next. Each chapter is like a story within itself. There are a variety of topics in the book, which will appeal to a diverse audience. Parker's very descriptive writing style paints vivid pictures of the many settings in which the story take place. The fanale presents the reader with a very unexpected and interesting twist.

Mitchell Mosher, DPM

Jack Parker has done it again. The second book in Parker's adventure travel series featuring Jeff Thornton and Trudy Garrison is a winner. The story, which takes place in the Patagonian region of Argentina, is exciting at every turn and the author's vivid description of the area makes the reader feel they are there.

Patagonian Adventure is a wonderful read for the entire family.

Marilyn Overhoff

To Deenise,
Happy 70th birthday!
With Warmest Regards,
Jack L. Parker

patagonian
adventure
book 2

patagonian
adventure
jack l. parker   book 2

TATE PUBLISHING & Enterprises

Published by Tate Publishing & Enterprises, LLC
127 E. Trade Center Terrace | Mustang, Oklahoma 73064 USA
1.888.361.9473 | www.tatepublishing.com

Tate Publishing is committed to excellence in the publishing industry. The company reflects the philosophy established by the founders, based on Psalm 68:11,
"The Lord gave the word and great was the company of those who published it."

Book design copyright © 2008 by Tate Publishing, LLC. All rights reserved.
Cover design by Stephanie Woloszyn
Interior design by Jacob Crissup

Published in the United States of America

ISBN: 978-1-60604-554-1
1. Fiction: Action & Adventure
08.07.07

Dedication

To Linda Bartlett, my sister-in-law. Thank you for your valuable suggestions and all your hard work.

Chapter 1

The screeching of the wheels, as the big jet came in contact with the surface of the runway, jolted Jeff Thornton and his father from the deep sleep they had fallen into a few hours before. It had been a tedious flight and a person can only talk or read for so long. Excitement probably had a lot to do with it in both their cases, but it was only after many hours in the air the Thornton's were finally able to drift off.

It all began one evening several weeks before. Jeff and his closest friend and next-door neighbor, Trudy Garrison, were doing homework. They had been taking summer courses at the local two-year college and were studying for finals. The shrill ring of the telephone interrupted their concentration.

"I'll get it," his father called out from the next room.

"Hello?" they heard him answer. "Yes, this is Thomas Thornton. Thank you, operator, I'll stay on the line." After what seemed like several minutes they heard a very surprised voice say, "Hello Mac, is that really you? It's great to hear from you. It's been a long time since we've talked. I guess you must have gotten my letter. Good. What do you think? Are you interested? That's great! When? Well, I think I can arrange that and yes I think he just might be able to come with me. Listen, let me check things out and see how long it will take to prepare and get a shipment ready for the amount you will need. When I do, I'll call you and we can go over the real details then. Yes, I understand. I know the telephone service in Patagonia leaves a lot to be desired but I will keep trying until I get hold of you."

At the mention of the word Patagonia, Jeff and Trudy's ears really pricked-up.

"Just where is Patagonia, anyway?" whispered Jeff to Trudy. "I don't know if I've heard of it. Maybe it's in Africa."

"No," she replied patiently. "Patagonia, at least the biggest part of it anyway, is located in Argentina. A small part of Patagonia is located in southern Chile."

Jeff was pretty sure Trudy would know where Patagonia was. Her father was a well-known travel writer and her mother a photographer. Trudy often accompanied her parents and at times their travels had taken them to some very remote parts of the world. She was a seasoned traveler by the time she was in her early teens. However, even though she knew where Patagonia was, she told Jeff she had never been there.

After his father got off the phone they could hear him talking to his mother in the kitchen where she had been cooking dinner. They could not make out the conversation, but they did hear his mother when she said,

"Oh, that's wonderful." Other than that they could not tell what they were saying.

Both of Jeff's parents are research scientists. At one time they had been working on a top-secret chemical. A chemical so frightening that if it had been developed and if it had ever gotten in the wrong hands, could have destroyed the world. His father had gone on a scientific expedition to the Himalayan Mountains. The expedition had something to do with there research. He had not returned and was presumed dead, killed in a plane crash high in the mountains. He was kidnapped by a Chinese Army Colonel named Chin. Colonel Chin wanted the chemical for himself. He was ruthless. With the formula he planned to gain control of the Chinese Army and perhaps, ultimately, the world. One year later Jeff's mother was abducted from their home and taken to Colonel Chin's secret headquarters in a very remote Tibetan monastery, the same place his father was being held prisoner. Chin needed both of them because they had been working on separate parts of the chemical. So, to get the formula completed he needed them both.

After his mother's disappearance, a Tibetan named Dorje approached Jeff. Dorje told Jeff he and some of his people knew about the plight of his parents and were going to try and free them. With the help of Dorje and his people, Jeff was able to play an important part in freeing his mother and father. Not only did this experience change his parent's lives, but his as well. Since their return home the laboratory where the Thornton's worked had closed and the project they were working on canceled. His parents had opened their own lab and vowed to direct their work toward projects that would benefit people, not harm them. Recently, they had finished developing a combination chemical fertilizer and pest control, a product totally harmless to humans and to the environment. It would replace or add any nutrients absent from the soil to grow whatever crop it was being used on and would eliminate only those insects or fungi capable of destroying the crop. It could be applied in several ways, by crop dusting from the air, by sprinkler system, or by means of irrigation. Possibly, its major attraction was the cost. It was very inexpensive and a small amount would go a long way. Jeff could tell by the excitement in his parents' voices when they told him about what they had just developed. They were very proud of their work.

Jeff and Trudy were just finishing what they were doing when Jeff's father walked into the room with a happy look on his face.

"Jeff," he asked, "how soon will it be before your summer classes are over."

"The middle of August," he replied, "just a little more than two weeks from now. Why, what's up, Dad?"

"Well," his father began, "how would you like to take a little trip with me."

"Where to?" replied Jeff, trying to act nonchalant. "Has it got anything to do with the phone call you had a little while ago?"

"Yes, as a matter of fact it does. You've heard me talk about my old college friend, George MacLean?"

"Yes."

"Well, Mac, as he is called, is from Argentina. He

came to this country to attend college to study agriculture. Actually, we were roommates and became fast friends. You know, even though we haven't seen each other for years, we still manage to write on a fairly regular basis. A few years ago his father retired and went back to Scotland to live and Mac inherited the family ranch in an area of Argentina called Patagonia. From what I gather from Mac, Patagonia in some ways is still like our old west. It is a big, lonely, and wild place."

"I know where Patagonia is," interrupted Jeff, "but only because Trudy told me."

"That's more than a lot of people know. Most of the people you would ask have never even heard of Patagonia. Anyway, Mac wrote me some time ago about wanting to grow his own feed for some of their cattle. It seems he raises both cattle and sheep, but his flocks of sheep and herds of cattle are all out on the range to feed. He wants to bring one of these herds in and feed the calves in pens. In that part of the country at least it would be strictly experimental. They do not grow their own feed, but allow the animals to forage on the range. I wrote him when your mother and I were close to developing our fertilizer and told him what I expected it would do. He wrote back telling me to let him know when we had finished our experiments and I did. The result was that phone call. He wants me to ship him enough to get started. I told him it had not been tested to any extent, but he said it did not matter. He was willing to give it a try. He has a son about your age and asked if you could come along as well. What do you think? Would you really like to go?"

"Would I!" Jeff blurted out, "When would we be

leaving? My summer classes won't be over for a couple more weeks, and I had planned on attending a series of special lectures the following two weeks. How soon would it be before we would have to leave?"

"There's a lot I have to do before we leave," answered his father, "but it looks like we will both have plenty of time. My guess is we won't leave until about the middle of October or at the latest the third week in October. I've got to make arrangements for shipping the material and I have to mix up enough of the stuff to do the job. That itself will take some time. The way Mac talked on the phone he wants enough to take care of at least a couple of thousand acres. If everything goes well I want to arrive down there at about the same time the fertilizer gets to his ranch. So timing is important."

After his father left the room Trudy looked at Jeff and said in a teasing voice, "Well, I guess it's back to school time. Just like before when you went to Tibet and you read as much as you could about it before you left. I think when we are finished with finals we had better get to the library and read up on Patagonia."

"I'm for that," he answered. "I certainly do not want to get down there and not know anything about the place. And I think I'll cancel out the lectures I was going to."

"Well, now you're finally getting smart," she kidded, and was really just as excited about the trip as Jeff was.

For a few minutes they just sat there deep in thought when a look of deep concern came across Trudy's face.

"What's wrong?" asked Jeff when he saw the look. "Is something wrong?"

"I just had this feeling come across me. And as you know, my feelings are very often right."

"What kind of feeling?"

At first she would not answer. Finally, though, she said, "The feeling that there may be some kind of danger in store for you. Now don't ask me what kind of danger because I don't know. Maybe its just kind of dumb, but I can't get rid of it. All I ask is you do me a favor and be very careful and don't do anything stupid."

"Trust me," he answered forcing a grin. "I promise you I will not do anything stupid."

Chapter 2

For the next two weeks most of Jeff and Trudy's free time was taken studying for finals. Jeff was able to squeeze in a few hours each week working at his parents' lab. Ever since they had opened their own laboratory, Jeff had worked for them on a part-time basis doing mostly janitorial-type work. After finals were over he and Trudy took a day to go fishing. They both loved to fly fish. Trudy made them a picnic lunch and they spent the day fly-fishing for trout on the little river, which runs not far from town. Jeff's father often fished with them and was invited but he was so busy at the lab getting things ready for Patagonia he did not have the time. In the morning, they found the fishing to be very slow. Even though they both fished hard neither one of them caught a fish. For some reason the trout were just not in a cooperative mood. While they were sitting on the banks of the river eating lunch, Jeff suddenly snapped his fingers.

"I forgot to tell you, but the other day I got a letter

from Dorje. He is probably coming for a visit sometime early next spring. My parents are really excited, and so am I. We really owe a lot to him. I don't know if I will ever fly in a helicopter again, but if I do, I sure hope Dorje is the pilot."

Trudy knew exactly what Jeff was talking about. She knew because Jeff's parents told her Dorje, another Tibetan named Bajay, and Jeff had freed them from the monastery where Colonel Chin was holding them prisoner. It was Dorje who piloted the helicopter they had stolen from the evil colonel. It was Dorje who flew them back to the valley where his people lived. The route they had to fly was through one of the most remote and dangerous parts of the Himalayan Mountains. The chances of even the most skilled pilot making the flight without crashing was very unlikely, but Dorje did it.

After their leisurely lunch they decided to fish until the early evening and then head home. That afternoon the trout, much to Jeff and Trudy's surprise, must have realized they were hungry. Jeff was fishing downstream from Trudy when he heard her give a sudden yell. He could see the deep bend in her fly rod as she skillfully fought the fish. When she brought it to her hand to unhook the fly from its mouth she quickly held it up for Jeff to see.

"How big," he called.

"A good fifteen inches," she called back as she gently released the fish and watched it swim away. It wasn't long before Jeff had a nice fish smack his fly. This time it was his turn to give a yell so Trudy could watch, as he was able to win the battle and then release his fish.

"How big was that one," she yelled.

"Not quite as big as yours, but it was still a pretty nice fish."

They had both caught and released several trout each and it was getting late. Jeff, who was walking upstream to find Trudy, found her standing in the water up to her thighs at the bottom of a long, smooth glide. On the far side, some time in the distant past, the trunk of a large tree had fallen into the river making the ideal home for a large trout.

"How are you doing?" he questioned as she stood motionless, her gaze fixed several feet in front of her at a spot where the current gently slid around the trunk of the tree.

"You won't believe this," she answered, her voice not much above a whisper, "but I just saw a fish rise right up there." She pointed with the tip of her rod. "By the size of the boil it made when it rose, it must be a big fish and I do mean big."

There was another boil on the surface, just as she finished talking, as the fish took another floating insect.

"Did you see that?" Jeff said wide-eyed. "You weren't telling a fish story because that is really a big fish. Why don't you wait for it to rise one more time so you can kind of judge its feeding rhythm? What pattern have you got on?"

"I've been using one of those flies we made up after the last time we fished. The one that looks like those big, gray mayflies that begin to hatch about this time of day. I saw a few floating in the current so I tied one on. I've caught my last three fish on it."

"That sounds good to me. I wouldn't change to a different pattern. I would use the same fly. I think that big brute will take it," answered Jeff, matter of fact.

They did not have long to wait before the fish rose again. This time they could actually see the insect the trout took. It was one of the big, gray mayflies.

Jeff knew if he were standing in Trudy's place, getting ready to cast to what might possibly be one of the biggest fish in the river, he would be very, very nervous. He felt Trudy's apprehension, but had the good sense to keep his mouth shut and let her do it all herself. Besides, he knew she was every bit as good a fly fisher as he was.

Trudy inched forward a few feet into a better casting position. Before making her first cast she wisely checked the fly and the knot that attached it to the leader. Everything seemed fine. The fish rose again. Trudy took a deep breath and began to false cast, lengthening out line trying to judge just the right amount she would need before she made the final cast. The slender rod flexed gracefully back and forth, back and forth making a swishing sound. The late afternoon sun glinted off the fly line. Jeff stood mesmerized by the poetic grace only an accomplished fly fisher can achieve. His father had taught them both the art. He had also taught them that catching fish was only a small part of fly-fishing.

"The most important thing about fly fishing," he said, "was the privilege to be able to be among the beauty of nature. Trout normally live in beautiful places. Catching fish is just a little more icing on the cake."

Trudy's first cast was short and just a bit too far to

the left. She glanced over her shoulder to see if Jeff was watching and he gave her a thumbs-up sign. She gave a smile in return as she began another cast. This time the fly landed softly as a thistle right where the current would carry it right over to where the fish had made its last rise. As the fly neared the crucial spot, Trudy's slender body tensed in expectation. On the bank Jeff stood frozen...waiting.

There it was, the bulge in the surface and the fly disappeared. Trudy's fly-fishing instincts took over. Her strike was the automatic reflex, which comes only after a lot of experience. The point of the hook penetrated into the tough, gristly part at the side of the fish's mouth; the perfect place. For just the shortest amount of time the trout did not react. Not uncommon when a big fish is hooked. When it did the smooth surface of the pool was shattered into a million particles of sparkling glass as the fish made a twisting somersault landing with a splash and immediately raced upstream. Trudy's reel screeching loudly in protest as the line began to melt of the spool. She knew if the fish was able to take off all the line it would break the leader. The only thing she could do to prevent this from happening was to follow the fish to try and gain back as much precious line as she could. There were only a few turns left on the reel when she began sloshing upstream after the fish. She held the rod high above her head with one hand and began reeling in line with the other. She was so engrossed with what she was doing she failed to see the rock, its top not quite above the water's surface. The toe of one of her boots kicked against it. Trudy pitched forward losing her footing. Try as she would, she was not able to gain her balance and went headlong into the water. It was when she was pitched forward she lowered the tip of the rod causing some slack in the line. The big fish broke the leader as though it was nothing more than a thin strand of a spider's web. Only a fisherman who has experienced a similar circumstance could know how Trudy felt.

The look on Trudy's face as she slowly waded to shore told the whole story. She was still reeling in her fly line when Jeff reached her side. Even though she was deeply disappointed, she did manage a week smile as Jeff took her hand and led her the rest of the way to dry ground.

"Look," Jeff began firmly, "it wasn't your fault you lost the fish. It was just plain old bad luck. You were doing everything right. Besides," he added, "just like my dad said, the time he lost that big trout. Do you remember? He said it was just a pleasure to have even hooked the fish. True, the one he lost wasn't as big as the fish you just hooked, but the saying still applies. And, look at it this way. To get as big as that fish was it had to be pretty darned smart. I'll bet it's seen hundreds of fake flies during its life and you were able to fool it into taking yours. Now, that in itself is something to be proud of. Plus, you know where it lives. Your day may come yet."

"You're right, at least I hooked that fish," she answered trying to smile as she began taking her water-filled waders off. "And like you said I know where this fish lives and I will be back."

"Anyway," Jeff laughed, "by the amount of water

you took in over your waders it's a wonder there's still enough left in the river to keep the fish alive."

"Ha, ha," Trudy dryly laughed, "you're really a smart aleck today aren't you? Besides, you of all people don't have any room to talk. It seems to me I can recall at least three times this summer alone when you have fallen in the river. Now, did I make fun of you when you fell in? I think not Mr. Jeff Thornton."

"All right, all right I am sorry, I was only kidding. I know it's no fun to fall in. Besides, since I hold the *falling in the river* record, I don't want you to take it away from me," Jeff teased.

"That is one record you can keep all to yourself. I know you were just kidding me. Actually, because it is such a hot day the cold water felt pretty good. Even so, I don't think I really want to make a habit of falling in, hot day or not."

That next evening Jeff and Trudy made a visit to the city's public library. It was time, they both decided, for Jeff to start learning as much as he could about Patagonia. Because Trudy had an inquisitive mind, she would study right along with him, just like before when he went to Tibet.

"Remember, how we had to cram to learn about Tibet before you left? At least this time you will have plenty of time," Trudy stated.

They decided to check out as much material as they could and go back to Jeff's house to begin. Jeff's mother was rather shocked when they walked through the front door, both their arms full of books. "I thought finals were over," she said with a rather puzzled look on her face.

"Finals are over, Mrs. Thornton," replied Trudy. "We went to the library to get some material about Patagonia so Jeff could learn as much as he could about it before he and Mr. Thornton left."

"What a good idea, Trudy," she replied. "It certainly is good to know something about any place you plan to visit. As you yourself know, it makes it so much more interesting. Well, I'll let you two bookworms get to work," she said warmly.

"Okay, where do we begin?" Jeff asked.

"I guess we should just pick a book each and begin," Trudy answered.

"Sounds good to me. I'll begin with this one," he said as he took a book off the top of the pile. Trudy took the next one down and they set to work.

They each had a notebook in which to keep notes and it wasn't long before they were both busy writing. After each had written several pages, Jeff's mother entered the room and asked if they would like a cold drink. They both answered yes.

"What would you like?" Mrs. Thornton asked as she began naming the various flavors.

"I'll take anything just as long as it's sugar free," answered Trudy.

"The same goes for me," came Jeff's quick reply.

In a few minutes Mrs. Thornton returned carrying two tall ice-filled glasses and two cans on a tray.

"How is the research going?" she questioned as she poured the liquid into the glasses.

"Pretty good," came Jeff's reply. "Of course some of the stuff I just read we learned in school, but then a lot of it, to me at least, is new."

"For instance?" asked Mrs. Thornton.

"Of course we all know the official language of Argentina is Spanish and the capitol is Buenos Aires," began Jeff by clearing his throat, "but I did not realize just how big a city it is or anything else about it until now."

"Well then suppose you tell both Trudy and myself about it?" his mother urged.

"All right, I will," he answered feigning smugness to his voice. "The Buenos Aires area has a population of about ten million people. This makes it one of the world's largest metropolitan areas. It is," he continued, "a very cosmopolitan city. The population not only of Buenos Aires, but Argentina itself, is made up of mostly Italians, Spaniards, French, German, and English. Like the United States, Argentina is a real melting pot settled by immigrants. Oh, and something else of interest, its seasons are just the opposite of our seasons."

"Not too bad, for a beginner anyway. I just wanted to test you," his mother said kiddingly. "Both of you keep up the good work. Now, I have some work to do myself," she said as she turned to leave the room.

"Jeff, have you read anything yet on the history of Buenos Aires?" asked Trudy.

"Yes," he replied, "I was just taking some notes about it when my mother came back with our drinks. You know, at first, I really only wanted to find out all I could about Patagonia, but when I began reading about Buenos Aires, I couldn't stop. It is really interesting. Do you know," he continued, "that the city was started by one of the first Spanish colonists, a guy named Juan de Garay? That was in 1580. Can you believe it, 1580? The city hall is still standing and so is the presidential palace, which is pink because they used the blood of cattle to make the color. Kind of gross, but I guess that's all they had, and the original plans for the city were drawn on the hide of a cow."

"While you've been reading about Buenos Aires," Trudy said, "I've been reading about the country of Argentina. Would you like me to tell you what I've found out so far?"

"You bet," Jeff answered.

"It is a pretty big country. It's the second largest in South America and about one-third the size of the United States. Now, I don't want to bore you with facts and figures, but I think you might like to know this stuff. Its total length is 2,360 miles, but its widest point is only 884 miles, which makes it a fairly long, narrow country. Now let me see," Trudy said reading her notes. "What else might be of interest? Oh, yes, Argentina is bordered on the south and west by Chile, on the north by Bolivia and Paraguay, on the northeast and east by Brazil and Uruguay. To the southeast is the Atlantic Ocean and the mighty Andes Mountains lie along the west and southwest border. The highest peak is Mount Aconcagua, which is 22,831 feet high. Now, that's a tall hill," Trudy said shaking her head.

Jeff, sat listening intently to what Trudy had been telling him. He appreciated her help, and in fact, was very interested in what she had been saying.

"Since it's getting late," he told her, "why don't we call it a night and get together again tomorrow night? I've got to work at the lab early tomorrow morning, but how about going for a jog with me in the afternoon when I get home?"

"Sounds fine to me," she replied getting up to leave. "I'll see you tomorrow afternoon."

"Okay, and thanks, Trudy. I really do appreciate your help."

"Well, what are best friends for anyway?" she said giving him a light punch on the shoulder with her fist.

Jeff opened the door and they gave each other a quick hug as they said goodnight.

Gosh, Jeff thought to himself, Trudy just barely comes up to my shoulder. I remember when we were both about the same height. I never thought I would ever get to be six feet two. Boy, we've sure been friends a long time.

He lay in bed thinking about how he and Trudy had first met. When her parents moved in next door, he had hoped they would have a boy his own age for him to play with. It was not to be. The first time he saw Trudy, it was a warm summer day and the movers had just finished unloading the furniture from their moving van and were driving away.

Jeff was standing in his yard when his new young neighbor came out and sat on the steps of her new home. She looked to be about his age. From the distance, though, he could not tell whether Trudy was a boy or a girl. She was dressed in blue jeans and T-shirt. Her short, blonde hair was cut in a style that would have fit either sex. But whatever it was, boy or girl, it looked lonely.

What the heck, he thought, only one way to find out.

Slowly, he sauntered towards her. When he was close enough, he could tell she had been crying, but he did not make fun of her as some might have done. Instead, he felt sorry for her. "Hi, my name is Jeff, what's yours?" he asked almost shyly. At first she did not answer. So he told her again what his name was, still not knowing whether she was a boy or not. "My name is Trudy," came the hoarse reply. He could still remember the disappointed feeling he had when he found out. A disappointment he tried hard to hide, but it did not take long for his disappointment to vanish, never again to enter his mind. That first meeting was the beginning of a friendship that has endured and would continue to endure. A friendship that to some might seem strange, but not to them. Now, they were both young adults and were still best friends.

Jeff was up early the next morning and after a quick breakfast was off to work. He rode his bike the two miles to the lab. Sometimes he would jog, but today he knew he would be running in the afternoon with Trudy, so he chose to ride his bike. He was in good physical condition. It had taken a lot of hard work on his part. He remembered how before he went to Tibet, he had to push himself to lose weight. How he had to work hard to get that muscle tone, to condition his lungs. If he thought he was in good shape before he went to Tibet, he was in outstanding shape when he returned home and he wanted to stay that way. He did not want to go back to the way he was. He had actually grown to enjoy exercising. Trudy, who was a natural at almost everything she attempted almost always went jogging with him. Normally, they would do about three miles, but today he thought they might push it a little and do five.

He saw his parents at the lab and they had lunch together. While they were eating, Jeff asked about how things were going with getting the chemical fertilizer mixed and ready for shipment.

"I think we are just about on schedule. It is a big undertaking and does take time. I just hope it does the job your mother and I think it will," his father answered.

"How long before it will be ready for shipment? And what will you do if it does everything you hope it will, what then?"

"To answer you first question, I think we will have everything ready and crated by the first of October. It will probably take a good two weeks to reach Mac's ranch, so I think we should plan on leaving no later than the middle of October. I will call him just as soon as the shipment is ready. He will tell me when to ship and then we can get a positive answer about when we will leave. Now, for your second question. If this stuff does all we hope it will do, what we will do then is to offer the formula to various companies for manufacture. We can't make it ourselves. It's all we can do to get enough ready to ship down to Mac. We will certainly choose very carefully the company we sell the formula to."

"Why," interrupted Jeff, "aren't they all about the same?"

"No. We want to go with a company that will still let us have some control. We want to be able to make sure they market it properly and are totally honest about what it will do. Also, we know it can be produced very cheaply and we want that to be passed on to the buyer.

After he got off work, Jeff rode straight home. He went to the phone and called Trudy who said she was ready to go. He said he would be over just as soon as he changed into his jogging shorts and shoes. In less than ten minutes he was knocking on Trudy's front door. She must have been waiting just inside because she flung the door open as soon as he began to knock, accomplishing exactly what she wanted to do—scare him half to death. They both laughed and Jeff pointed his finger at her and said he owed her one.

"I think we'll jog to the river and take the trail that leads downstream to where you hooked the big trout, turn around and backtrack home. How does this sound to you?" he asked Trudy.

"Sounds good to me," she said, "but the trail does get a bit rough in places. I don't want either one of us to twist an ankle."

"If we have to, we'll slow down to a walk when we get to the rough places. I don't want either one of us to get hurt, either."

After doing some stretching exercises, off they went. Jeff knew Trudy could keep up no matter what pace he set, but because it was a very warm day, the pace he set was nice and easy.

It was a good feeling he had as he and Trudy ran side by side. As he often did, he could not help thinking just what a true friend she was. She has always been there for me, he thought to himself, even during those hard times when I did not know whether or not I would graduate from high school. Through all my problems, she never deserted me. I know I can always count on her and I hope she knows she can always count on me. That's what friendship is all about.

When they reached the river, they left the road, and started on the trail. When they came to the rough spots, Jeff would slow down. There were a few places where they did have to walk, but over all, it wasn't bad. They were nearly to the pool where Trudy had hooked the big trout, when they heard the scream.

Chapter 3

They stopped and looked at each other with their mouths wide open. Before either could say a word to one another, an even louder earth-shattering scream split the air. Without a second thought, they raced up the trail in the direction the screams were coming from. As they rounded a sharp bend, they saw a young woman standing on the edge of the river frantically looking into the water. It was the very same pool where Trudy had lost the big trout. They ran to her side and asked what was wrong. The woman was beside herself, but was able to tell them her little boy had been wading in the shallow water just at the edge of the river. She had only turned her head for as long as it took to get her sunglasses out of her purse. In that short period of time he had disappeared, vanished.

"Only one thing could have happened," stated Jeff. "He must have waded out into deeper water and was sucked under by the current. The tree, Trudy, the tree! He may be caught underwater in the branches of the tree," Jeff shouted as he began wading frantically towards the fallen tree. Trudy was right behind him and they dove under the water at the same time. They did not have to dive a second time. Not far in front of them, in the deepest part of the pool where the branches were thickest, they could see the limp body of the little boy laying hopelessly tangled in the tentacle-like prison. They forced their way through the underwater forest to the boy's side. Jeff took hold of his arms while Trudy fought to tear the branches away so Jeff could pull him free, their lungs crying for oxygen. With the boy free, they literally popped to the surface gasping for air and swam holding the little one between them. It was only a few strokes before they were able to touch bottom. With an added burst of strength they reached shore. Jeff, who now cradled the boy in his arms, immediately laid the child on his back. Trudy placed her fingers on the side of his neck and said she could feel a slight pulse. Jeff tilted the head back, lifted the chin, and opened the mouth to make sure there was nothing obstructing the airway. It looked clear so he pinched the nose so it was closed, and at regular intervals began to blow air into the child's mouth. Seconds passed with no response. A few more breathes and it happened.

"Look, look, his eyelids are fluttering," Trudy whispered breathlessly. At almost the same time, there came a heave of his chest as he began to breathe, followed by a cough. Jeff quickly turned the little guy on his side as the water that had been in his lungs came gushing out of his mouth. When the little boy began to cry, the mother who had been standing close by as though she were in a trance, came to life and she began to shout,

"My baby, my baby, he's alive, he's alive." But the fight was not yet won. There was the danger the child could go into shock. Trudy ran and snatched up the blanket the mother had laid out on the sand and she and Jeff wrapped the small boy in it for warmth.

"Do you have a car?" Jeff asked the mother who was now so engrossed in her baby she did not answer. "Do you have a car," he repeated loudly.

"Yes," she answered in a quivering voice.

"We have got to get your son to the hospital," said Jeff sternly. "Take us to your car, now!"

Jeff's last words seemed to snap the young mother back to the situation at hand and she said to follow her, the car was parked just up on the road.

"Do you have the car keys," Trudy asked as they hurriedly followed her. "Yes, I do. They are in my pocket."

"Give them to me," Trudy told her, "I will drive to the hospital."

When they saw the car, Trudy ran ahead, opened the doors and started the engine. Jeff and the mother sat in the back seat, with Jeff still holding the little boy and told Trudy to take the back way to the hospital, because it would probably be the fastest way. "We should be there in just a few minutes," Jeff said trying to console the mother, "and look, the little guy has stopped shaking and his color is certainly a lot better."

Trudy drove right to the emergency room entrance, stopped, jumped out of the car and ran inside. She grabbed the first nurse she saw and quickly explained the situation. At that point, Jeff burst in carrying the little boy with the mother at his side.

. . .

The nurse took the baby from Jeff, told the three of them to sit down and wait, the baby was in good hands and disappeared through a closed door.

Jeff and Trudy sat trying to reassure the mother, who, at this point, was not even able to cry, only stare at the floor. They did get her to tell a little about herself and her little boy, whose name was Joshua, and was almost three years old. It seemed she and Josh were just passing through, saw the little river, and because it was such a warm day, she decided to stop and let him play in the water. Jeff and Trudy could tell it was very hard for her to talk, but she took a deep breath and continued. "My name is Lois Fields. My husband was killed six months ago in a freak accident where he worked. Like I said, Josh and I were just passing through. We were on our way to my parents in another part of the state to stay with them until I got a job. Well, anyway, you know the rest. If I would have lost my little boy, too, I just don't know what I would have done. I certainly have not shown it, but I am so very grateful to you both. Words just cannot express how I feel."

"We were glad we were close enough to be able to help," Jeff told her. "Oh, by the way, my name is Jeff and this is my friend, Trudy." It was at that point a tall man wearing a long white coat came through the door and walked towards them.

"I'm Dr. Sims," he said with such a big smile on his face, words were hardly necessary. "Who is the mother of the little boy?" he asked kindly.

"I am," Lois replied nervously.

"Well, I am happy to say he is going to be just fine. We do want to keep him overnight, but only because we want to keep an eye on him."

When she heard the words of the doctor, she broke down and cried. This time, though, the tears she was shedding were tears of joy, but hers were not the only tears being shed.

The three of them followed the doctor through the door into a large room, past several curtained off cubicles and through another door into a smaller room in the far corner with a single stretcher-like bed in it. Joshua lay on this bed with two nurses, one on each side. When Joshua saw his mother, he sat up, held his arms out to her and said, "Mommy, I'm hungry."

The mother and her now very alert son, were totally engrossed in each other. Trudy tapped Jeff on the shoulder and made a motion that they should probably sneak out and leave them alone.

When they were standing outside the hospital, Trudy said to Jeff, "Boy, what a terrible time Lois is having. Can you imagine how much more difficult it would have been for her if she would have lost Joshua after losing her husband only recently? I don't even want to think about what it would be like. It's no wonder she was almost a basket case through this whole thing."

"Like I told her," began Jeff. "I'm really thankful we were close by so we could help. It really makes you feel good doesn't it?"

"You bet it does, you bet it does," answered Trudy with a tone of deep sincerity in her voice.

"Hey, I don't know about you, but I think I would rather walk home than jog."

"Sounds good to me," replied Trudy, "my knees are still shaking."

When they reached Jeff's house, nothing was said to his parents about what had taken place that afternoon. Trudy's parents were off on an assignment and would not be back for another two weeks. As she normally did, when she did not travel with her parents, Trudy was eating at Jeff's house. Trudy went home to clean up and was back in plenty of time for dinner. She and Jeff cleared off the table and loaded the dishwasher. When they were finished, Jeff asked Trudy if she would like to get back to the books? "Tonight I want to try and find out as much as I can about Patagonia," he said firmly.

"Fine with me," she said. "Let's get to work."

The only noise from either one of them for the next two hours was the sound of turning pages, writing, and the occasional hum, as one of them discovered something extra interesting. Again, it was Jeff's mother who broke the silence when she came into the room and said, "Okay, you two, knowing you would probably be burying your noses in those books again tonight, and knowing from past experience how thirsty it makes you, I made some lemonade.

"Now," she continued, feigning her expertise at making lemonade. "This is not lemonade from a can. No sir. I squeezed the lemons myself this afternoon when I got home from the lab. By now it should be ice cold. Do I have any takers?"

They both raised an arm and said very loud in unison, "Yes!" as the three of them laughed.

"You know, Jeff," Trudy said after his mother left the room, "we sure are lucky to have the parents we have. Even though both your parents are research scientists and they both have a PhD, some people might think they would be different. You know, kind of weird, the nutty professor type, but they act just as normal as my parents or for that matter the same as any good parents would act. I am sure glad our parents are such close friends. I feel very lucky because I really have two sets of parents, my own and yours. Your mother and father have always treated me like a daughter."

"You know something," Jeff said, "that is exactly how I feel too."

"What have you two been talking about while I was gone," Jeff's mother asked when she came back into the room.

"Nothing at all, Mother, nothing at all," he answered as he and Trudy smiled at each other.

Setting the tray with the pitcher of lemonade and three glasses on a table, she poured the ice-cold liquid into each glass.

"I thought I would join you, so I brought myself a glass. Do you mind?"

"Well I guess we will let you stay, especially since you worked your fingers to the bone making us this delicious lemonade," Jeff kidded as he smacked his lips.

"Why thank you both," she answered as though she was being granted a great privilege. "I want to hear what you two have discovered tonight about Argentina. I guess one is never too old to learn as the old saying goes."

"Would you listen to her, Trudy? The way she talks you would think she was one hundred years old. By the way, not to change the subject, but where is dad tonight?"

"He had to go back to the lab and do some work. He left when you were both hard at work in the kitchen doing dishes. He told me to tell you goodbye. He did not want to ruin your train of thought."

"Like Dad said, things are going according to plan at the lab."

"So far so good. Even though it's a long, hard process and a lot of work, like he told you, you will probably be able to leave by the middle of October," answered his mother.

When Jeff's mother stated the date he and his father would be leaving for Patagonia, for some reason Trudy felt this foreboding feeling pass over her like a dark, unwanted shadow. Her body visibly shuddered.

"Trudy, what's wrong?" Jeff's mother asked, deeply concerned when she saw Trudy's reaction to her statement.

"Nothing, nothing is wrong. For some reason I just had a chill, that's all," Trudy replied in a rather weak voice.

"I hope you're not catching a cold."

"No, I'm alright," Trudy said reassuringly.

"Well, let's get on with it. What have you two brilliant young people learned so far this evening?"

"Tonight," replied Jeff, "we both thought we would focus our attentions on Patagonia."

"Let me see, last time Jeff had the pleasure of going first, so Trudy, how about you being first tonight?"

"That's fine with me," Trudy answered, "I would love to go first. It seems the explorer Ferdinand Magellan and his men were probably the first Europeans to set foot in Patagonia. That was in 1520. Magellan's ship anchored just off shore from what is now the town of San Julian, a pretty desolate area even today so you can imagine what it was like way back then. It was on a very windy day when they set foot ashore. One of the first things they saw was a set of footprints. These were not your average footprints; these were enormous in size. They were so enormous it scared the heck out of the landing party and they turned right around and rowed as fast as they could back to the safety of their ship. They did not want to come face to face with whatever or whoever owned such huge *patagones,* which means big feet. Especially in such an ominous looking land. Even in those early times, it seems it did not take the story of the 'big feet' long to spread throughout the civilized world. What kind of humans lived in the land that seemingly stretched westward to where the sunset? This was the land that eventually became known as Patagonia. That is how Patagonia got its name, at least this is the most popular of the stories of how it was named."

"Did they ever find out about the kind of people who had such big feet?" asked Jeff's mother.

"They were probably made by Araucanians. The Araucanians were the Indians who lived in Patagonia. They were a very tall, grim, and fearless people. Today, they are called Mapuches after the language they speak. Most of the lakes and rivers in Patagonia have Mapu-che names. Sadly, though, there are not many Mapu-che's left."

"Trudy, that was very good," complimented Jeff's mother, "I will give you an A for your part of the report. Jeff, what do you have to add?"

"I'll start off with another famous explorer, Sir Frances Drake. In 1578, he made a short stop in Patagonia, but he was not interested in exploring the area. The reason he went ashore was to hang one of his officers. I assume this officer had committed some kind of serious crime. I read Drake even had breakfast with the officer before he was hanged."

"That seems really gruesome," stated Trudy, with Jeff's mother nodding her head in agreement.

"I agree," said Jeff. "I guess they did things differently in those days. I wonder what he did to deserve being hanged?"

"I wonder if the poor man even had any kind of a trial," stated Jeff's mother. "I guess like you said, Jeff, things were sure done differently in those days. I don't think I would have wanted to live in those times. I don't think life meant very much. Go on Jeff, I'm sorry I interrupted."

"Well, let me see, how about the climate? For its latitude anyway, the climate in Patagonia is not too bad. The summers are fairly cool and winters pretty mild, but it can get very hot in some parts, as well as very cold, and boy, the wind can and does really blow. The scenery seems to be pretty wild. In the most southern part of Patagonia there are a lot of glaciers. From the picture I got while I was reading, this place called Patagonia is a lot like Wyoming here in the states. There seems to be a lot of huge, wide-open spaces with sagebrush, very few trees and not many people at all. The Andes Mountains though have a lot of forests, lakes, streams and rivers—basically the Andes are just about like many other mountains in the world. Would you believe there are still unexplored areas of Patagonia?"

"Have you found out anything on how big an area of Argentina, Patagonia really is?" questioned Trudy.

"As a matter of fact I have," Jeff answered proudly, "Patagonia, is a pretty darned big place. According to what I have just read, it is as big as the combined states of Texas and Ohio. It certainly is much, much, bigger than I thought it was. I mean just the state of Texas itself is a big chunk of land. Add the state of Ohio and just think of what you've got."

"So far it's an A for each of you," stated his mother. "Now I'm going to leave you two to your studies. Oh, by the way, I won't see either of you until dinner tomorrow night. I have to make a trip to the city and I will leave early in the morning. I'm going to talk to a women's club. I guess one of the members read the article, which was written about our work in the Farm Journal. Actually, it's a garden club and they want me to give a talk about the new fertilizer we've developed. I'm pretty excited because we want the average gardener to know about and use it, not just the farmer and rancher."

"That's great," Jeff and Trudy said in unison.

"I think it's time I went home," Trudy said. "I'm tired and I want to get to bed early."

"That sounds good to me," agreed Jeff, "I have to go into the lab pretty early tomorrow to work. I think Dad wants me to start bagging the fertilizer he has ready so far to be shipped. I guess when he has enough mixed to make it worthwhile, that's what he will want me to do. That way it won't all have to be done at once. That should certainly make it a lot easier for me. When he feels he has the proper amount, and it is ready to go, he will call his friend in Argentina. From the lab it will go by truck to the coast and then by ship to Buenos Aires. Anyway, it looks like I'll get a pretty good workout tomorrow."

The next day Jeff did get a workout, but he was through before lunchtime. His dad said he was done for the day and could leave. When Jeff asked his father he said he would be home for dinner. He had worked late the previous night and did not get home until well after midnight and was back at the lab early the next morning before Jeff.

When Jeff arrived home, there was a note from Trudy saying she was off doing errands. So, after a quick lunch he thought he would do a little more research on Patagonia. After a good forty-five minutes of reading and note taking, he heard Trudy at the front door. "What are you doing?" she asked when she walked into the room.

"Since you weren't home and I had nothing else to do," he replied, "I thought I would do some more reading about Patagonia, and man did I ever find out some great stuff."

"What do you mean? What kind of stuff?"

"You know, the more I read about this place the better it sounds. What I have just finished reading is about Mike Cassidy and Robert Parker."

"Mike Cassidy and Robert Parker? Who the heck are they? I've never heard of them."

"Well then," answered Jeff, "do you recognize the names Butch Cassidy and the Sun Dance Kid?"

"You mean to tell me," Trudy said in a surprised voice, "Mike Cassidy and Robert Parker are the real names for the famous western outlaws, Butch Cassidy and the Sundance Kid?"

"You bet I do. I didn't know their real names myself until I read it in this book," Jeff said as he handed Trudy the book he had been reading.

"It says here," Trudy read, "the cabin Butch Cassidy and the Sundance Kid lived in is located near a place called Cholila, Patagonia, which is very close to the Chilean border, and it is still standing. I wonder if you will be going anywhere near that?"

"I haven't got the slightest idea," Jeff said, "but if it is, I sure would like to pay the place a visit. I guess I'll just have to wait and see when I get there."

"Cholila, must be in the Patagonian province of Chubut," stated Trudy, "because it says here, Butch Cassidy and the Sundance Kid went to the director of the land a little department when they got to Buenos Aires and applied for, and received 12,000 acres of land in Chubut. They worked the ranch with Eta Place, who was the girlfriend of the Sundance Kid, and three others, for about two years. They must have gotten bored with ranch life after the hectic and dangerous life they had lead as bandits out in our west, so they began a new life of crime in remote Patagonia. The true story of what really happened during that time is really not very clear at all. However, the police were pretty hot on their trail, so they sold their ranch in 1909 and just kind of vanished. Of course, the rumors flew, but what really happened to Butch Cassidy and the Sundance Kid is not known for sure and probably never will be."

"I gather from what we have read so far," Jeff surmised, "Patagonia is still pretty much the same wild, desolate, and remote place it was when Butch Cassidy and the Sundance Kid lived there."

"I agree," answered Trudy.

"You know, not to change the subject," Jeff said, "but I was just thinking. I haven't been on a horse since I got back from Tibet. The place Dad and I are going to is a real ranch, right? Ranches usually have horses. So, I thought we might start going a couple of times a week out to your parents friends' farm to ride their horses like we used to. What do you think? I would really like to be in shape for riding when I get down there. It sounds like the horse is still a pretty important mode of transportation in Patagonia."

"That sounds good to me," Trudy replied enthusiastically. "You know how much I love to ride. Anyway, I haven't been out there since the last time we rode together. I'll give them a call and see if it's all right, although I know it will be because they don't ride much and they appreciate our exercising their horses. I can hardly wait. In fact, I'll go call right now."

Trudy went into the next room to call and was back shortly, wearing a big smile. "We are always welcome to come out and ride anytime we want. We don't even have to call beforehand. If they are not at home we can still ride. We know where everything is. 'Make yourselves at home,' she said."

"That's great," Jeff said. "When do you want to go?"

"How about right now?" Trudy answered. "I can run home real quick and change and it only takes us about fifteen minutes to drive out to the farm. We would have a good two hours to ride before we have to be back for dinner."

"That sounds good to me. You go home and change. While you're gone I'll change and write a note telling my mother where we've gone and we will be back in time for dinner. Mother said she would probably be home from the city in the early afternoon."

"Good, because I told them we would be out this afternoon."

.   .   .

Jeff stopped the car at the front door of the big, white-framed farmhouse. Trudy got out and returned shortly after talking to the farmer's wife. She told Trudy they were very pleased to have them ride just as often as they wanted. She did caution her saying the horses might be a little frisky, because it had been some time since they had been ridden.

The two horses were enclosed in a small pasture out behind the barn. With the aid of a couple of apples as an enticement, it wasn't hard to catch and lead the horses into the barn where the saddles and bridles were kept. Trudy always rode the little gray mare and Jeff, the larger chestnut mare. The horses certainly were feeling full of energy and Trudy had to hold each horse, in turn, while Jeff placed the heavy western saddles on their backs. It wasn't long before they were ready to go and led the horses out of the barn so they could mount up. It had been so long since they last rode the horses; Jeff totally forgot his horse had the bad habit of inhaling air when the saddle was placed on its back. This caused its abdomen to become larger than normal. What he should have done was let the horse settle down and let its breath out, which would result in the abdomen going back to its normal size. When Jeff tightened the cinch he did not realize the horse had taken in a breath and had not let it out. As he prepared to mount by putting his left foot in the stirrup and pushed off with his right so he could swing into the saddle, the horse let out its breath. Now, of course with Jeff's weight in the stirrup, the cinch was too loose to hold the saddle in place. His right leg was about halfway over the horse when the saddle came sliding off the horse's back. Jeff landed flat on his back. The ground where he landed was soft, so other than his pride, he was not hurt. The horse stomped its front hooves, gave a whinny, turned its head, and gave Jeff a look as if to say, *well you dumb cluck it serves you right. I hope you've learned something here today,* and shook its head several times.

Trudy, who was already on her horse, jumped off and ran to Jeff's side and helped him slowly to his feet.

"Are you all right?" she asked anxiously.

"Yes, I think so," came his shaky reply. "But I feel pretty darned stupid."

"I'm sorry, but now that I know you're okay, I have to laugh and agree with you, because you really did look pretty stupid."

"Go on, laugh all you want. I deserve it. I should have known better."

"I'm just glad this did not happen while we were out riding. If the saddle would have rolled off then you really might have been hurt."

The horses settled down shortly after they began their ride and seemed to enjoy being out as much as Jeff and Trudy. For Jeff, being in the saddle brought back pleasant memories of Hercules, the horse he was given to ride after reaching Dorje's secret valley in Tibet. As he and Trudy slowly rode along the scenic country roads he told her about Hercules and how good it felt to be on a horse again. He also told her about how he doubted he would ever ride a horse equal to the magnificent Hercules. The thought, not only of the horse, but the far off valley, its warm, friendly people and what they had done for Jeff and his parents brought pangs of sadness to his heart. Jeff told Trudy how much he missed them. Trudy understood how he felt and said she, too, was glad to be on a horse again. In about two hours they headed back to the barn. After unsaddling the horses they walked them around the barnyard for about ten minutes, gave them a good brushing, checked their hooves to make sure they had not picked up any rocks from the trail, and turned them loose in their pasture.

• • •

Later, as the four of them sat down to dinner, Jeff's mother told them her talk had gone even better than she had expected. She said she would do the dishes and

Jeff and Trudy should get on with their research on Patagonia.

They had just started reading when they heard Jeff's father go out the front door to get the just-delivered local evening newspaper from the porch. Following his usual routine, he opened the paper to check out the front page before going back into the house. It was the headlines that caught his eye and caused him to let out a low cry of disbelief. Instead of going to the living room to read the paper he walked straight into the kitchen where Jeff's mother was. Neither Jeff nor Trudy paid any attention to the muffled conversation coming from the kitchen. It was Trudy who glanced up first to see Jeff's parents enter the room. Each of them wore a look of grave concern on their face.

Chapter 4

"Jeff, Trudy, can you please tell me where you two were yesterday afternoon?"

"Sure, Dad," Jeff answered. "We jogged out to the river. And, speaking of the river I forgot to tell you about the really big trout Trudy hooked the other day on a dry fly—"

"That's great," his father said interrupting, "but did anything happen? Was there anything unusual that might have happened to you when you got to the river. Your first names are Jeff and Trudy aren't they?"

"Of course those are our first names, Dad, but I don't understand; is there anything wrong?"

"No, I don't believe anything is wrong," replied Jeff's father. "But I am a little puzzled and so is your mother. We are puzzled by what the headlines and this article say here in today's newspaper. Here, you two read it."

Jeff took the newspaper his father handed him and held it so Trudy could read it, too.

Plastered across the front page was the headline: *Two Teens Save Drowning Child.*

The article began:

The search for two young heroes known only as Jeff and Trudy goes on. If you know of two young adults, in their mid-to late-teens who go by those names, please contact local officials.

There was a phone number and the article went on describe how the child was saved. There was also a statement from Dr. Sims, the emergency room doctor who was on duty, which said, "There is no doubt in my mind the quick and efficient way Jeff and Trudy reacted to this terrible situation is definitely what saved the child's life. Not only would the grateful mother like to thank them, but myself and the rest of the emergency room staff who were on duty."

When they had finished reading, Jeff and Trudy gave each other a wide-eyed look in stunned disbelief. "Gosh Dad, we didn't think we did anything anyone else in our position wouldn't have done. We just happened to be there at the right time to help. Once we got to the hospital and we found out the boy was going to be okay, we just kind of slipped out and came on home."

"That's right," added Trudy. "When we found out Joshua, that's the little boy's name, was going to be fine, we didn't want to be in the way. We were just thankful everything turned out the way it did."

"Well, you two, and I know I speak for both of us, when I tell you what you have done and the manner in which you acted makes us even more proud of you."

Jeff's mother who had remained silent said, "I don't think any parents could be any more proud of the both of you. Trudy, I know when they find out, your parents will feel exactly the same."

These last statements by his parents caused Jeff and Trudy some embarrassment. Both Jeff and Trudy knew his parents did not mean to embarrass them, but only wanted them to know how they felt. Jeff would have like to drop the subject then and there and continue on with their studies, but his father told them they must call the newspaper first thing the next day.

When his parents left the room, Jeff agreed with Trudy, when she told him she hoped people were not going to make a real big deal out of what they had done.

Next morning, with Trudy at his side, Jeff phoned the newspaper and told them who they were. "Yes, yes, yes," he kept repeating to the questions he was being asked. "You say it won't be more than a few minutes. Yes, we will wait right here until you call back," he answered giving the phone number. "Whoever I was talking to on the phone is calling the mayor. After he's talked to him, he's going to call right back."

When the call came, Jeff answered after the first ring. "Wait just a minute," he replied after a short conversation. "Trudy, they want to know if we can come down to city hall tomorrow at three o'clock in the afternoon? The city wants to give us some kind of award. What do you think?"

"Okay," she said, "but tell them we do not want a lot of fuss or anything. We will get the award and then that will be that."

"We will be there. Yes, so will my parents, but Trudy's are away on a business trip so they won't be able to attend. No, there is no way we can contact them. My parents will fill in for her parents."

Jeff then called his parents at the lab. He explained to them what the city wanted to do for them and when. He told them they said they would accept the award providing there was not a lot of unnecessary fuss about what they had done. Those were the terms Jeff had stated and they were agreed on.

His parents said they would certainly attend and agreed with Jeff and Trudy's wishes, and they asked Jeff to tell Trudy they would consider it an honor to act on her parents' behalf.

.   .   .

It was the next afternoon and nearly three o'clock. Jeff and Trudy were standing on the steps of the town's small city hall nervously waiting for his parents. A wave of relief swept over them when they saw their car drive up. Jeff's parents lead the way. Since opening their lab they had been to city hall many times and knew exactly where to go.

The four of them were ushered, without delay, into the mayor's office by his friendly secretary. She introduced them to the mayor, who walked out from behind his desk to greet them. There seemed to be a genuine sincerity in his manner. They immediately felt at ease with this man. He told them the presentation was to be held in the meeting room down the hall and asked if they would please follow him. They were taken down a hall to a set of closed, double doors. When the doors were opened they were surprised at what they saw. Just inside the door stood a small crowd of people. At the very front stood Joshua and his beaming mother. Behind them were Dr. Sims, and all of the emergency room staff who had been on duty the day Joshua was brought in. Jeff and Trudy stood frozen with their mouths open, unable to speak. Jeff's parents were also at a loss for words. It was Joshua who broke the ice when he looked at them and said. "Hi, my name is Josh. My mommy told me what you did for me. It would have been really bad for her if I weren't around anymore, cause she really needs me to take care of her. Besides, I'm big enough, don't you think?" he added puffing out his chest.

"You bet you are," Jeff and Trudy answered with deep sincerity.

As they had requested the ceremony was brief and not in the least bit embarrassing. First, Dr. Sims said a few words, followed by the mayor, who presented Jeff and Trudy each with a gold plaque and framed certificate. They were given the highest honors for bravery the town could give. A photographer from the newspaper took pictures. The presentation was not a hurried affair, just to get it over and done with. No, it was done with the greatest respect. During the proceedings, Jeff's parents stood close behind them, their faces beaming with pride.

After it was over Joshua's mother, Lois, took them aside and gave each a warm hug and some good news. While Joshua had been in the hospital, she checked out their bulletin board for job opportunities. There was an opening for a position in the office she felt she was qualified for. She then applied, and got the job.

"Yes, things certainly are looking up for Josh and myself," she told them with a misty-eyed smile.

In the evening, Jeff and Trudy went for a bike ride. More than anything they just wanted to get away for a while and be by themselves. What they had actually done had begun to sink in. Before, they nearly accepted what they had done as just another routine act of daily living. Now, they were aware of what they had done—they had saved a life. Jeff and Trudy, each in their own way, felt very humble and thankful for being granted this privilege.

The next day's newspaper carried a nice article about Jeff and Trudy, and the award they had been presented. They were pleased with the article and even admitted the photo the paper used of them was pretty good.

The following few weeks were relatively normal for Jeff and Trudy. Jeff worked most mornings at the lab for his parents. Often, in the afternoon, when he had finished his class, he and Trudy went out to the farm to ride the horses or go jogging. Several times they rode their bikes out to the river to fish. Of course, Trudy had hopes of hooking the big trout again, but she was not successful. Several of their evenings were taken up with their further studies of Argentina and Patagonia. Trudy's parents returned from their assignment and were just as proud of their daughter and Jeff as any parents could be. It was Jeff's parents who told them about Jeff and Trudy rescuing young Joshua from drowning, and about the honors the town had given them. It seemed only a few days, before they were off on another assignment to still another part of the world. They wanted Trudy to go with them, but she declined, saying she wanted to stay home and keep Jeff's mother company while Jeff and his father were away in Argentina. Jeff's mother knew how much Trudy loved to travel and tried to talk her into going with her parents, but she would not budge from her decision. Finally, one night, Jeff's father phoned his friend Mac in Patagonia. It seemed like an hour before the call was finally completed.

"Everything is ready to ship," his father said. "Just give me the word when to do it."

"As soon as possible," came the reply. "We are ready down here."

"I can have it loaded on the trucks by day after tomorrow and it should be at the dock and loaded on the ship within the week. I have made prior arrangements with the shipping company. I talked to them this afternoon and this arrangement will work out just fine. They have a ship in port now and it leaves for Buenos Aires at the end of the week. The next ship they have scheduled for Buenos Aires is not for another month. Boy, you talk about perfect timing."

"Good thinking, my friend. You and your son are welcome to come anytime now."

"Well, it's almost the middle of October so I think if we can get a flight, we will leave probably about the same time the ship does. We will get down there several days before the shipment, but that will give Jeff and I some time to have a look around Buenos Aires before we come on down to your ranch. I will let you know as soon as we get our tickets. Does this sound good to you? Do you have any suggestions?"

"No, I have no suggestions," came the reply. "I think you will both like Buenos Aires. Anyway, I am certainly looking forward to seeing you again and meeting your son."

Chapter 5

The jet taxied slowly towards the terminal. The Thornton's looked at each other and smiled. Finally, they were in Argentina.

The flight from the US had taken them through two time zones. They had crossed the Caribbean Sea, the Amazon Basin, and Gran Chaco before landing at Ezeiza Airport, which is located about thirty minutes from downtown Buenos Aires.

Checking through customs went smoothly and it wasn't long before they were piling their luggage in a taxi and were on the way to their hotel.

When they left home, it was autumn. The trees had begun to turn their deep crimson and gold and the nights were crisp. In Buenos Aires, it was spring. There was balmy warmth in the air and here the trees were deep green, with new leaves.

At the suggestion of his friend Mac, Jeff's father had made reservations at a hotel in the central area of Buenos Aires. The hotel was located just one block off the famous Avenue Florida. The Avenue Florida is closed to all but foot traffic, and is one of the city's most famous downtown shopping areas. It is often crowded, not only with shoppers, but with those who are there just to be seen.

The route to the hotel took them down wide, tree-lined streets lined with ornamental old apartment buildings with balconies filled with plants. Yet, often next to these would be a new apartment building, but it too would have its plant-filled balconies. The number of parks they passed especially pleased Jeff. He saw joggers and people sitting on benches or at tables playing games or just talking. When they went down a narrow, cobblestone side street, the driver had to slow down because a group of young boys were playing soccer.

After the rather hair-raising ride in the hot taxi, it felt especially good as they walked into the cool, marble-floored lobby of the hotel.

After unpacking and freshening up they felt pretty good. They talked it over and decided, because it was early in the evening, they would have plenty of time to walk around and check out the local sights and do some shopping for themselves as well as for gifts to send home. In Argentina, like in many countries of the world, the evening meal is normally not eaten until around nine in the evening or later.

On their way out of the hotel, they stopped at the front desk to ask where they might do some shopping and where they could find a good restaurant to have dinner. The pleasant desk clerk told them they were only one block away from one, if not the best shopping area of Buenos Aires—the Avenue Florida.

"It is," he said, "lined with wonderful shops of all kinds. There are boutiques, leather goods shops, bookstores, and art galleries. You will find just about anything you might want on Avenue Florida. There are also many cafes where you can relax and take a break from shopping. However, might I suggest a small shop just off Avenue Florida? It has the best buys in the city," he added, "for Argentine handicrafts. Anything you buy, we will wrap and ship for you here at the hotel to any part of the world. And for your dinner, located not far from this shop is a restaurant I am sure you would enjoy. They serve traditional Argentine meals, and even though it is often crowded, you should have no problem getting a table. Wait just a moment, and I will draw you a map." When he had finished Jeff's father took the map the clerk handed him, thanked him and they walked out of the hotel towards the Avenue Florida.

Because it was open to foot traffic only, there were no cars to contend with on the crowded avenue. For this, they were especially glad, because they had discovered on the taxi ride from the airport just how fast the Argentines drive.

"Yes," the taxi driver told them, "we drive very fast, but with great skill." The pace of the avenue they found was slow. You did not come here to hurry. They walked, browsed, people watched, and admitted to each other they were really having a great time even though they were shopping—something back home neither one really liked to do. Like the desk clerk told them, the shops along Avenue Florida had something to offer for almost anyone. There were shops of all kinds; some of them were located in shopping malls with openings on Florida and the adjacent streets. This really was a shopper's paradise.

"Wouldn't Mom and Trudy have a great time here," Jeff said to his father who rather grudgingly agreed as they checked out the goods on display in one of the trendy shops. They looked at each other and broke out laughing.

They were in a bookstore, just kind of browsing through the English language section, when Jeff's father looked at his watch.

"It's getting kind of late," he told Jeff, "so if we want to check out the shop the desk clerk told us about we had better head that way. I really wonder if it is a good as he said it was. Oh, well, let's go have a look."

Before they left the bookstore they looked at the map they had been given. "It looks like we are about here," the elder Thornton said, pointing his finger at the map. "So, we don't have far to go."

"That sounds good to me, Dad. I'm beginning to get a little hungry. I guess by the time we finish at this place it will be time to eat our dinner. By then I'll probably be so weak from going without food for so long I don't know if I'll have enough strength to get to the restaurant."

"You wanna bet?" his father kidded.

The shop was everything they had been told. The shelves and display cases were full of Argentine handicrafts. This was not a shop for the unsuspecting tourist, full of junk. The stuff in this place was the real thing. The knowledgeable salesperson that waited on them said the handicrafts they offered came from the different provinces of Argentina. It was hard to decide, but they ended up buying beautiful hand woven wool scarves for Jeff's mother and Trudy. When they were shown some leather handbags they bought each of them one of these as well. For himself, Jeff had to have a wide, gaucho belt with silver inlay. His father, with a little urging from Jeff, bought a landscape painting done in watercolors. They were told the artist, whose name was Tomas, was a gaucho whose rather primitive style was just beginning to be noticed by collectors. This particular scene was of an area in the Patagonian province of Chubut.

"The packages," said the salesperson, "will be wrapped and delivered to your hotel by noon tomorrow."

"That's great," Jeff replied. "Now we don't have to carry all of this with us to the restaurant."

His father agreed, and seemed just as glad as Jeff.

As they were about to leave, they named the restaurant and asked how far it was they had to walk. "It is only a few short blocks," the salesperson replied, "and may I add, you have certainly made a good choice. The food is excellent. I am sure you will like it. It is one of the best parrillas in the city."

"What is a parrilla?" asked Jeff.

"It is what you might call a steakhouse in your country. Here in Argentina, we eat a lot of beef."

The smell that can come only from the cooking of good food hit them as soon as they walked in the door. The restaurant was crowded, but they only had a short wait before they were taken to a table by the window. When they were seated Jeff said, "Gee Dad, this restaurant smells great. I think even if I had just finished one of Mom's great special occasion dinners and walked into this place I would be hungry all over again."

His father smiled and nodded his head in agreement as he studied the menu.

After awhile they decided they needed some help. The waiter was very patient as they asked what many of the dishes on the extensive menu were. When Jeff asked what a bife de costillo was, and the waiter replied it was a very large T-bone steak, this is what Jeff said he wanted to order. His father chose a bife de chorizo, after the waiter explained it was a thick steak cut from the underside of the rib roast. When the food arrived even Jeff was a bit taken back by the amount that was set down before them. The steaks were the biggest he had ever seen. Along with the steaks, each had a huge pile of crisp, French fries, and a green salad. It only took a couple of bites before Jeff told his father it was the best steak he had ever eaten. The elder Thornton said he could only agree as he took another mouthful. It took quite awhile, but finally, their plates were almost empty. After each had eaten the last little morsel, Jeff's father said he did not think he would ever be able to eat again. He was that full. Jeff, though, at the suggestion of the waiter, did have enough room left for a dessert of baked custard. It was so good he said he wished he had enough room for another, but had to admit he didn't.

They walked slowly back to their hotel. By the time they got there some of the fullness had left them.

The wake up call they had asked for came right on time. Jeff wanted to go jogging and was told there was a very nice park not more than a few minutes walk from the hotel. His father would eat a little breakfast while he was gone and then pay a visit to the office of the shipping company to check up on when the fertilizer would arrive. He knew Mac had already made the arrangements for the cargo to be shipped from the port to his ranch, but he wanted to check things out just to make sure there were no snags. They would meet back at the hotel and go to lunch together.

The park was easy to find and Jeff was pleased to see several joggers there ahead of him. Even at this fairly early hour it was pleasantly warm and several people were sitting at tables playing chess. After a long, leisurely jog, he headed back to the hotel. After taking a shower, he had a quick breakfast and went for a walk. When he arrived back at the hotel his father was waiting for him.

"How did things go at the shipping office?" he asked.

"It looks as though the shipment is right on time. It seems it was almost delayed by a storm at sea, but according to the person I talked to at the shipping office, the storm veered off in another direction at the last minute so it wasn't a problem after all. We fly out three days from now and it should be pretty close behind us."

That afternoon and the next two days, the Thornton's played tourist. They visited museums, art galleries, and did some more shopping. They found Buenos Aires to be the perfect city for walking and they walked as often as they could. Both came to the conclusion, Buenos Aires was not only beautiful and cosmopolitan, but it was also full of warm, friendly people. The combination was perfect and very rare, especially in such a large place.

Their flight was to leave at midnight. They took a short nap and were up by ten at night. Since they had already packed, they figured this would give them plenty of time, because they did not have to go to the same airport. Ezeiza Airport, where they had landed when they arrived in Argentina, is the international airport where all foreign flights land and leave from. Because they were flying to a destination within the country they would be leaving from, Jorge Newberry Airport, which is located in the city. This airport is used mostly for local flights and was only a short drive from where they were staying.

After a quick bite to eat in their room, they went down to the desk to check out. "Your taxi is waiting and your luggage has been loaded," the desk clerk told them. As they were about to get in the taxi, Jeff suddenly had this feeling deep inside him. It was a rather confusing feeling. He could not tell if it was from excitement or the feeling he had had in the past; the feeling that some kind of danger lay in his future. Jeff knew, the feelings were closely related, so it was hard to tell.

The plane left right on time. The flight to their destination in Patagonia took several hours. Even though neither he nor his father had had much sleep, Jeff was wide-awake for the flight, while his father slept peacefully in the next seat. Once they left the lights of Buenos Aires behind it looked like they could be flying over a black void. The earth below was that dark.

The uppermost rim of the sun was making its appearance on the horizon when the plane began its approach to land at the small, rural airport. In the dull, gray light of the new day, Jeff was just able to make out the almost treeless landscape below.

"Patagonia," he muttered " I wonder what you have in store for me?"

Chapter 6

Even though most of the seats on the plane were empty, Jeff let the other passengers sharing the flight leave the plane before he woke his father. Normally, a very sound sleeper, Jeff was surprised at how quick his father reacted to the gentle pokes on his shoulder.

When they left the plane they walked towards the only building they could see, their shoes made crunching sounds on the gravel of the runway. The building looked more like an oversized wooden shed. They stood outside with the small group of fellow passengers waiting for their luggage to be unloaded from the plane. Finally, a man and young boy came around the far corner of the building pushing a large, flat cart. A couple of the males in the waiting group walked out to the plane with them. When the door of the luggage compartment was opened, the others boosted the boy up so he could climb inside. His job was to slide the various bags and packages to the edge of the door so the others could stack them on the handcart. When everything was unloaded and stacked it took all four of them to push the cart on the graveled surface to where the rest of them were waiting. The man opened the door to the building and the three men formed a line. The cart was unloaded by handing each piece down the short line to be placed on the floor of the shed. Now it was the boy's turn. He would push the bags across to the middle of the floor and placed them in a straight row to make it easy for the passengers to find their own baggage. When the cart was empty and the luggage placed in position, the passengers were told they could claim what was theirs. Everything was done in a very orderly manner. There was no pushing or shoving. As soon as someone found what belonged to them, they would carry it out the front door of the building. Jeff wondered what they were going to do next, when a small, rather rickety bus drove up in a cloud of dust. When the luggage was piled on top and secured, the people boarded. When everyone was seated, the bus took off down the road causing an even bigger cloud of dust.

The inside of the building was totally quiet. Only Jeff and his father remained. There was a small desk in the far corner and a few chairs along one wall.

"Well, Dad, what should we do now?"

"Wait. Mac said he would meet us and he will."

They had just sat down when the back door opened and the man and the boy who unloaded the plane walked in.

"Hello, my name is Thomas Thornton and this is my son, Jeff. We're supposed to be met here by a friend, but it looks like he hasn't arrived yet. His name is

MacLean, George MacLean. Do you happen to know him?"

"Certainly. Everyone knows him. The MacLean's are a fine family and well known in not only this part of Patagonia, but all of Patagonia. But, they have many miles to travel and because of a strong tail wind, your plane was early. So, perhaps he will be here soon."

"What happened to the crew of the plane," Jeff asked, "we haven't seen them since we landed."

"They are in the plane taking a nap," the man replied with a grin. "They have a return flight to Buenos Aires in three hours."

"Is this your son?" Jeff asked pointing to the boy.

"Yes," replied the man proudly, "this is my son, Frederico. During the week he is in school, but on Saturday's and school vacations, he helps me out here at the airport. He is a very hard worker. My name is Frederico, too," he added.

"Nice to meet you both," answered the Thornton's, which caused the boy to smile self-consciously.

"Ah, I think your friend is coming," the boy's father said looking out the front window. "I can see a cloud of dust on the road and it seems to be coming this way. It is too early for anyone taking the next flight to arrive, so my guess is, it is George MacLean."

Both Jeff and his father stood up and looked out the window as a Range Rover pulled to a stop in front of the building. Both the driver and passenger were blond, taller than average, and it did not take a second look to tell they were father and son. After stretching their arms they walked towards the door.

"That's Mac. That's him all right. Even though I

haven't seen him for all these years, I'd know him any-where. The only thing different about him is, he's put on a little weight and his hair is thinner."

The MacLean's both stood in the doorway their eyes adjusting to the dim light as they looked around the room. It was Jeff's father who walked forward with his right hand held out. It was met with a firm grip from his old friend. At first they just stood in silence shak-ing hands, looking at each other. Still, without speak-ing, they released their hands and wrapped their arms around each other while Jeff, the younger MacLean, Frederico, and his son all looked on with respect.

Next, came the introductions.

"This is my son, Jeff."

"This is my son, Roberto, but call him Robert."

After some small talk Mr. MacLean, walked over to Frederico's son and reaching in his pocket pulled out a small paper bag and handed it to the boy.

After the boy gave his father an anxious look the father said it was okay for him to accept it. A broad white-toothed grin lit up his face as he thanked Mr. MacLean for the gift.

"Candy, candy," he cried showing his father. The boy then went to each one of the others offering to share, before he even took a piece for himself.

"Well," Mr. MacLean said, "we had better get started. I thought because we have a pretty long drive ahead of us, first we would have some breakfast in the village."

"That sounds fine with us, doesn't it Jeff?" answered Jeff's father as Jeff eagerly nodded his head in agree-ment.

They piled their ample gear into the back of the Range Rover, said goodbye to Frederico and his boy and drove off down the dusty road.

In just a couple of minutes they came to the top of a hill. Not far below, tucked away in a small valley and surrounded on three sides by shaggy hills, lay a small, tidy-looking village. At the edge of the village a tree-lined river snaked its way towards the flat, empty desert. They drove slowly, past neat one- and two-story houses, each with its colorful bed of flowers. In the business section, Mr. MacLean pulled up in front of a brick building sitting by itself on a corner and told them this was the restaurant where they would have breakfast.

Jeff noticed there was still just a little bit of chill in the air as they walked towards the entrance. Inside, the few customers greeted both MacLean's and they in turn greeted each of them by name. The MacLean's introduced Jeff and his father and the greetings were warm and friendly. They were made to feel welcome. The Thornton's did not feel one bit out of place, and the food certainly smelled good. The four of them ordered steak and eggs. When the food was set in front of them, even Jeff knew he had a big job ahead of him.

Jeff and Robert had taken an instant liking to each other. While their father's talked of old times, Jeff thought he would ask Robert a few questions. He began by asking how big their ranch was.

"Well," Robert began with a friendly grin, "to begin with, here in Argentina, they are not called ranches like they are in your country. Here they are called estancia. But you can certainly call it a ranch if you want to. And, to answer your question, our ranch covers more than one hundred thousand hectares. A hectare is equal to almost two and a half acres."

"Wow, that's one heck of a lot of land. How do you take care of that much land?"

"My father employees many men, because besides the land, we have more than twenty thousand sheep, several thousand head of fine cattle, and more than two thousand head of horses, plus, we raise polo ponies as well. Argentina is very famous for polo. It takes many gauchos to take care of the sheep and cattle and several campanistas to take care of the horses."

"I've read about your gauchos and know they are like our western cowboys, but what are campanistas?"

"You are right about the gauchos, because they are in many ways like the cowboys of your west. The campanistas are what you would call horse wranglers because they look after and train the horses. However, each gaucho also has his own string of horses to ride and take care of."

"On the drive from the airport I couldn't help but think about the state of Wyoming back in the US. I have an uncle who lives there and we've gone to visit him on vacations. Patagonia, at least this part of it anyway, looks a lot like many parts of that state, kind of semi-desert, sage brush, not many trees, miles of flat areas, some hills and rugged cliffs with mountains in the distance."

"If that is what Wyoming looks like, then you are pretty close. This part of Patagonia, in fact, much of Patagonia must be very similar to Wyoming."

After they finished eating, Robert's father looked

at Jeff and his father and asked how they liked their breakfast?

It was Jeff's father who looked at Jeff and said, "Well Jeff, why don't you answer that question."

"Okay, I will. I think I speak for both of us when I say this has been one of the most delicious and filling gastronomical adventures we have ever experienced," he said breaking into a laugh and hastily added. "Really, though, it was even as good or better than any of the breakfasts we had in Buenos Aires." To this his father heartily agreed.

"Since it looks like you two have had enough to eat," Robert's father teased, "then, I guess we had better get on the road, because like I said, back at the airport, we have a pretty long drive ahead of us."

After they left the village behind, Jeff said to Robert, "How long will it take before we get to your ranch, oh, sorry, I mean estancia?" he asked correcting himself.

"It depends."

"What do you mean by it depends?"

"If everything goes alright and we don't have a flat tire or a rain storm doesn't hit us or we don't have to stop to help someone in trouble along the way, we should be there in about three hours."

"Is the village where we just had breakfast the nearest to your estancia."

"Yes."

"Man, Patagonia really is a big place, isn't it?"

"Yes, it is a very big place. You see the northern border of Patagonia is the Colorado River, which is over eight hundred miles from Buenos Aires. It is more than twelve hundred miles from the Colorado River to the southern most part of Patagonia. We live in the central part of Patagonia, in the province of Chubut. The Argentine part of Patagonia covers over three hundred thousand square miles. Barely four and a half percent of the population of Argentina lives here in Patagonia. So, it is not only big, but not very many people live here either. I hope," he continued, "I'm not boring you with all of these facts and figures, but I thought it was probably the best way for you to get a mental picture of how big a place Patagonia is."

"No, I don't mind you throwing stuff like that at me. I really am interested. By the way, how do you know all of this, anyway?"

"We learn it in school."

Mile after mile, the sometimes twisting, but mostly straight gravel road, took them on a slanting course towards the rugged, snowcapped Andes Mountains. Occasionally, they would pass flocks of sheep, watched over by one and sometimes two horsemen. More than once, Robert's father had to bring the vehicle to a stop, while a small sea of bleating wool crossed the road. They were always moving in tight formation, because of the hard-working sheep dogs. When the gauchos rode past, they would always wave a greeting, and they would wave in return. Jeff was impressed by the way they seemed to always sit so straight in the saddle. A couple of times they crossed small streams on rather rickety bridges.

"These may not be much more than trickles of water now, but they can become raging torrents during times of rain," Robert told him. The larger streams were crossed on much sturdier bridges where swarms of purple-colored swallows darted through the air chasing insects. To Jeff, the larger streams looked like they might hold trout, but he did not ask.

The road never seemed to end. On their left was the flat, barren, windswept desert-like expanse, broken only rarely by sparse stands of poplar trees. Sometimes a small building or house could be seen in among the trees. In the far distance, the desert seemed to have no end. Instead, it just melted away into the dim, gray horizon. On their right, the direction the road now began to take, Jeff could see a range of hills and far behind them the ever-present bulk of the Andes. He became mesmerized. He had fallen under the spell of the passing Patagonian landscape. The range of hills now turned into a series of jagged, multi-colored sandstone cliffs, split here and there by narrow canyons. For a short distance, the road climbed steeply to a stretch of green grass-covered plains, dabbed here and there in various colors from an artists' palette by large clusters of wild flowers. Grazing among the wild flowers were several flocks of sheep. At the far edge of the plain was a pile of tumbled, black hills. Once over these, they dropped down onto another larger grass and wild flower plain. There were no sheep on this plain, but Jeff could see many various sized herds of cattle. Across the plain, the road followed a beautiful, clear flowing river. There were more trees now. Large sections of the foothills were heavily cloaked in forest. In some places the forest seemed to extend all the way to the very base of the mountains. This, Jeff realized, was a truly spectacular place. One mountain seemed to stand out above all the others, because of an umbrella of clouds that never seemed to change. Robert told him the mountain was an extinct volcano that for some reason almost always had a formation of clouds hovering just above its top.

Jeff mentioned to Robert about the cattle being the first they had seen since leaving the village. He explained to Jeff that Argentina raised some of the finest beef in the world and was one of the world's leading exporters of beef. He went on to tell him most of the beef was raised up north in the area known as the Pampa, and while most of the animals raised in Patagonia were sheep, this area did raise a fair amount of beef. His father, at present, was trying to build up their herd of fine cattle. This was why he was going to try and raise his own feed. And the reason Jeff's father was asked to help in the experiment was because of the combination chemical fertilizer and pest control he and Jeff's mother had invented.

"Do those happen to be some of your cattle?" asked Jeff pointing out the window.

"Yes, those are part of our herd."

"That looks like a lot of cows to me. Do you still have more?"

"Oh, yes, we have a lot more cattle. That is just a part of the herd."

When Robert was finished talking, Jeff happened to glance out the window at the sky. What he saw caused a low whistle to escape from his lips. A bird, a very big bird, its huge wings fully outstretched was lazily drifting above. It stood out even more because of the deep blue of the cloudless Patagonian sky, which served as a backdrop. Even the eagles he had seen in Wyoming were not nearly as big as this bird. He asked Robert to look up where he was pointing.

"What kind of bird is that, Robert? I didn't know anything that big could fly."

"That's a condor." Robert replied, "There are a lot of them in this part of Patagonia."

"I've heard of them and seen pictures of them, but I didn't realize they were that big. How do they get off the ground, anyway?"

"They have to face into the wind either from a cliff where they can sail right into the air or if they are on the ground they have to run downhill into the wind so they can get up enough speed so they can take off."

"When I first looked up and saw it, I thought it might be someone in a hang glider. That's how big it looked."

Jeff's last words brought a big grin to Roberts face.

They both became silent. Before long, Jeff became just as absorbed in the passing scenery as before, and he began to think about his new friend. He seems to be about my age," Jeff reasoned. "Really level-headed and I feel as though we have known each other for a long time. It's seems kind of like we're old friends, not two guys who just met for the first time only a few hours ago."

A gentle nudge on the shoulder from Robert woke Jeff from his thoughts.

"We are almost there," Robert told him with a tone of excitement in his voice.

Jeff did not know what to expect and certainly was not prepared for the sight that greeted his tired eyes.

Chapter 7

Jeff had closed his eyes for a while and hadn't noticed a few miles back when they turned off the main road and were on the drive leading back to the estancia. Mr. MacLean stopped the vehicle at the top of a hill that was just high enough to give them a good view of what lay below. The scene spread out before them caused both Jeff and his father to blink several times in amazement. They had no idea it would be anything like what they were seeing.

"Well, there it is," declared Mr. MacLean, with a sweep of his arm. "This is our estancia. I want to make it very clear right now that we want the both of you to feel completely at home while you are here. Our casa is your casa, as the saying goes, and we really do mean just that."

The first thing to catch Jeff's eye was the house. It was big, made of adobe brick, with two stories and a bell tower. Poplar and pine trees surrounded it. Beds of bright, multi-colored flowers bordered the acre-sized green lawns and the sun reflected warmly on its red tiled roof. Not too far from the main house were other varied kinds of buildings and corrals. Largest among these looked to be a huge barn. It was all very neat and tidy, and a very impressive sight.

Coming down off the hill, they turned onto a circular drive and stopped in front of the main entrance to the house. They had no more than gotten out of the vehicle, when one of the double doors opened, and a smiling, elderly looking woman walked spryly towards them.

"This is Nina," Mr. MacLean said introducing Jeff and his father. "Nina is our housekeeper, but she is much more than that. She has been on the estancia all her life, and like many of those who work here, is like one of the family. My wife and Robert's younger sister are visiting relatives in Scotland, and won't be back until just before Christmas, so Nina really looks after and takes care of us."

When Jeff began to unload their luggage, Nina, gently slapped his hands and told him to leave it alone, she would send someone right out to bring it up to their rooms.

Inside, the house seemed even more impressive than it did from the outside. While their fathers were busy talking, Robert gave Jeff a quick tour of some of the downstairs part of the house. The living room ceiling was two stories high, and crisscrossed by heavy, exposed wooden beams. From the living room, Robert led Jeff into the library. Even though, it too, was a large room, it had the feel of warmth and comfort so often found only in smaller rooms. A generous sized desk sat in front of French doors that looked like they lead out onto a patio. The walls of this room were lined with shelves full of books. There was a long, library table located along one of the walls of the room with plenty of space for the ladders, which moved on tracks, so you could easily reach even the highest shelves. There were several leather chairs grouped around a fireplace, which was almost as big as the one he had seen in the living room. Maybe it was because he loved books that Jeff really felt comfortable in this room. Next, they went into a long, well-lit room Robert told Jeff was the gallery. On each of its three walls hung the estancia's large collection of paintings. Robert said his grandfather was an art collector and so were both his parents. The way Robert talked, it seemed the whole family appreciated art. Robert mentioned, too, that one of the gaucho's who worked on the estancia was even gaining quite a reputation as an artist. The outside wall of the gallery was a series of almost floor-to-ceiling windows with a set of French doors, which led onto the same courtyard or patio as the library's doors. Looking out, Jeff could see a large fountain in the middle and rows of blooming flowers around the edges. There were several chairs and some tables placed near the windows where you could relax and enjoy the paintings and the view outside. Robert told Jeff they often had breakfast and lunch in the gallery. Next, because time was running short, Robert took Jeff upstairs to show him his room. When they walked through the door, Jeff was surprised to see all his luggage neatly stacked at the foot of the large, heavy wooden bed. The room was spacious. Because of the many windows and a set of French doors that opened out onto a balcony, it was also bright and cheer-ful. When he walked out onto the balcony, he saw he was standing just above where the doors of the gallery opened onto the courtyard.

"Pretty nice," complimented Jeff. "Pretty nice. I think...in fact, I know I will like this room."

"Jeff, I hope you understand, when my father said he wanted you and your father to feel at home, he meant it. So, whatever you do, please do not feel you have to ask first. Treat this just as you would if it where your own home."

If Jeff had not felt relaxed before, he certainly felt relaxed now. When they had first driven up in front, he had some twinges of doubt about how at ease he would be staying in what back home would be called a mansion. However, that feeling had now completely disappeared.

Robert left Jeff to unpack his things, telling him he would come and get him when lunch was ready. He had just finished his unpacking, when there was a knock on his door.

"Come on in," he called out, "the door is unlocked."

"It looks like you've been pretty busy," Robert said when he came into the room. "Are you ready for some lunch? It should be ready by the time we get down-stairs."

"I'm always ready to eat," answered Jeff with a laugh. "And as you can see I've got all my stuff put away and the room is now as neat as when I first got here."

During lunch, Jeff's father told him, because he

and Mac would be so busy during much of their stay, he would be in the very capable hands of Robert.

"Your father and I," Mr. MacLean said, "will be spending a lot of time where the planting is to be done, which is near where we have built the new pens for the cattle."

"Where is that?" questioned Jeff.

"About ten miles from here. Because the estancia is so large, we have several places where we have gaucho's living. Of course, right here is considered the main headquarters. The others are what you might call satellite headquarters. We felt the best place for our experiment was the one I just mentioned. Water here in Patagonia can be very scarce. We are very fortunate because the estancia is blessed with an abundance of water, underground as well as many streams, one of which is large enough to be a small river. After lunch I want to take your father to where we have prepared the ground for planting and get his opinion. Even though he and I will be very busy during your stay, we do have some things planned while you are here, but I will let Robert tell you about that later."

After they finished lunch, Robert asked Jeff if he would like to take a tour of the grounds.

"Would I? That would be great," he answered enthusiastically.

First, Robert took Jeff to the huge barn he had seen from the hill. Robert told him it was their stables. Inside the stables he took him to the office where he introduced him to their capataz, or foreman, Tomas, and some of the other gauchos who worked on the estancia who were in the office as well. They were all in the traditional gaucho dress of baggy, pleated pants, wide leather belt with lots of silver decorations, and stiff brimmed hat. Jeff noticed that each had a large silver handled knife in a sheath stuck into the back of his belt. Their handshakes were firm and sincere.

"Wow," Jeff thought to himself, "these guys are a pretty tough looking bunch. I sure hope I can stay on their good side."

Although it was hard to tell, Jeff judged Tomas to be in his late 60s. He was about medium height, slight of build, and stood ramrod straight. Jeff felt right off the bat that here was a man who was born to be respected. Even though he seemed to be all business, Jeff did notice a sparkle in his dark eyes; and the kind of smile suggesting he probably had a heart as big as the world, a man who would go to any lengths to help a fellow human being.

The gauchos were sitting around on boxes and old chairs in a loose circle and it was Tomas who said, "You are just in time, Robert. We are just about to have our maté. Perhaps, you and Jeff would like to join us?"

"Maté, maté. What is maté?" Jeff quickly whispered to Robert.

"Maté is kind of like regular tea, but it is made from the leaves of a shrub grown in northern Argentina and in Paraguay. Almost everyone in Argentina drinks maté. The closest thing to what it tastes like, so I have been told anyway, is very strong Chinese green tea. True, for someone who has never tasted it, it does take getting use to, but you really should give it a try."

"Sure, what the heck. If I could learn to like yak

butter tea in Tibet, I think I can learn to like maté in Patagonia."

"Tomas," Robert said, "we would like very much to drink maté with you."

"Good, the water is boiling," replied Tomas smiling, as he walked over to the corner of the room and took a blackened kettle with steam pouring out its spout off a small stove. Jeff watched with interest as Tomas poured the boiling water into the orange-sized gourd, he had filled just before with green leaves. After replacing the top, a silver straw was inserted through a hole in the top and the gourd, which Jeff noticed was partially encased in a design made of silver, was handed to him.

"This is quite an honor for you, Jeff," Robert said. "To be the first to drink the maté. Now, what you must do is drink all the maté. When you are finished hand the gourd back to Tomas. He will refill the gourd with boiling water and hand it to the next person."

"Okay, here goes," Jeff said as he took his first sip through the straw. "Man, that is hot, but you know, it does not taste bad at all. In fact, I like the taste. And you were right, Robert, it really does taste like strong Chinese green tea."

When he had finished his maté, he handed the gourd back to Tomas. Tomas, refilled the gourd with boiling water, but did not remove the maté leaves and handed it to Robert. When he had finished, it was Tomas' turn and so on down the line, until everyone had had their turn. When the last gaucho was finished, only then were the leaves emptied out of the gourd.

"I guess the first one to drink the maté gets the

strongest tea," Jeff said to Robert after they said good-bye to the foreman and his men.

"Yes, that's true. So, naturally after each gourd, the drink gets weaker. Like I told you, to be given the first gourd of maté is an honor. I think you made a very favorable impression, not only on Tomas, but the other gaucho's, too. This is not so easy to do. However, the way you drank your maté, believe it or not, was very important, and I've got to tell you, you drank it as though you had been drinking it all of your life."

"Like I told you, if I was able to learn to drink yak buttered tea in Tibet, well let me tell you, maté in comparison is like drinking ice cold homemade lemonade on a hot summer day. But do you know something, I really got so I looked forward to the yak stuff, especially after a really rough day on the trail, and believe me, every day on the trail was rough. That's when it actually tasted good, plus, it gave you back your strength… that strength you had to have to go on. You could just feel it kind of creep up through your whole body. It was really something."

"Then you really were in Tibet?" Robert asked impressed.

"Yes," Jeff replied, "I was, and sometime, if we have the time, I'll tell you a little about it. Anyway, what is this we're standing in? It looks like some kind of really big horse barn."

"You're right, it is a horse barn, and yes, it is pretty big, isn't it? In this barn we keep nothing but polo ponies."

"Polo ponies. Do you mean you weren't kidding me

this morning when you told me you raised polo ponies?" interrupted Jeff.

"No," replied Robert with a laugh, "I was not kidding when I said we raise polo ponies. Do you know anything about polo?"

"No, not really. I do remember reading somewhere, though, polo is a very physical sport and a good polo pony can be worth an arm and a leg."

"I don't know about being worth an arm and a leg," Robert answered, "but even an average polo pony is worth a lot of money. The better the pony, of course, the more it is worth. The best ponies are worth a lot of money. We raise polo ponies not only for ourselves here on the estancia for our own team, but also to sell. We have the reputation of raising some of the best polo ponies in Argentina. We have sold ponies not only here in this country, but all over the world."

"How many polo ponies do you have here on the estancia, anyway?"

"I'm really not sure how many we have right now, I would have to ask Tomas, but I know we have more than two hundred."

"Two hundred. Wow! Even I know that is a lot of polo ponies. Do you mean to tell me you can sell all of those horses?"

"Not really, because that figure includes our stallions, brood mares and colts. Only a certain number of ponies are ready to be sold at one time. And, like I told you we have ponies for our own team to ride. Before you ask, I'll tell you, yes, we have a polo team here on the estancia."

"Okay, then, how long does it take to train a polo pony?"

On the average, it takes about four years."

"How are they trained, anyway?"

"Part of their training consists of working the pony with a cow."

"I don't understand, what do you mean working with a cow?"

"A single cow is placed in a corral. The pony works the cow back into the corner of the corral. The rider does not even touch the reins; he lets the pony do it all. What it does is teach the horse to react very quickly, and they also become very sure-footed. Believe me," Robert continued, "you would not want to be playing polo on a pony that tends to be clumsy. The sport is dangerous enough, even on the best of ponies."

"That's another thing, why do they call them ponies?" asked Jeff. "Aren't they the same size as a normal horse?"

"Yes they are. At one time the size of the horse was limited. I think it was in about 1919 when this rule was changed. The ideal size, though, for a polo pony is fifteen to fifteen and one half hands high. A pony any bigger than this might not have the quickness needed. But, then again, there are always exceptions, and even though the horses are bigger today, they are still referred to as ponies."

Next, Jeff asked if a polo pony was a special kind of breed, like a quarter horse or Arabian?

Robert told him that in Argentina, their polo ponies were a cross of the original horses brought by the early Spanish explorers and the English thoroughbred. He said it seemed to be the ideal cross for a polo pony. He went on to tell Jeff, he was not bragging, when he told him Argentina breeds some of the finest polo ponies in the world.

"The best ponies," Robert said matter of factually, "can sell for as much as one hundred thousand American dollars."

"What! Did you say what I think you just said?" Jeff blurted out.

"You heard right. I did say one hundred thousand American dollars."

"I think I will start raising polo ponies," Jeff kidded.

"I only wish it was that easy," replied Robert, "but it isn't. It takes a lot of money to get started and it can take many years before you sell your first pony."

"Oh well, I can dream can't I?"

They began to walk down the long, fairly wide hall that separated the individual closed boxes or stalls on each side of the barn. Each one, Robert told Jeff, housed a pony. The not unpleasant smell of horses and fresh straw mingled together, filling the air. Every so often a soft whinny or a horse stomping its hoof could be heard behind a stall's closed door.

"Come over here, Jeff, and I will show you a polo pony. Like I said, all of the horses in this barn are polo ponies, and they are all fully trained. Many of them are the ponies we ride when we play, but several are going to be sold. We hold a yearly auction here at the estancia to sell our ponies. It is by invitation and buyers come from all over the world to bid on them. It is a very exciting time. It lasts for a whole week and among other things there are several games of polo played to show the buyer how good the horses are. There is a lot of food, cooked by the gauchos, and everyone really seems to have a good time. The gaucho's play some of their traditional games and put on a rodeo. It is really a very big thing in this part of Patagonia and many of the gauchos who attend come from many miles away. Some of the other estancia's bring horses to sell and of course we play each other in polo."

"That really does sound exciting," Jeff stated. "When does it begin."

"In less than a month. Hopefully, you and your father will still be here."

"That's great, because the way my dad talked, we will be here longer than that. But tell me how do all of these people get here and where do they stay when they do get here?"

"The invited guests fly into the same airport you did. Buses from the village bring them out here to the estancia, and as you know, it is a pretty long trip, but nobody seems to mind. Even though the buses are a lot bigger than our vehicle, the drivers tend to drive pretty fast so it takes them a little less time to get here than it did us. We set up a series of tents for the invited guests, but they are not just ordinary tents, they are actually pretty fancy. Now, the gauchos ride here on horses and camp out just as though they were out on the open range. Everyone, in the area is welcome to attend. This is really a kind of relaxed and fun-filled time for everyone, except at the auction for the ponies. With the addition of the other estancia's who come and bring their ponies, there is usually about two hundred offered for sale."

"Do they sell them all in one day."

"No, the auction takes place the last three days of the week, after the polo matches have all been played."

"You said all the horses here in this barn were already trained polo ponies, well, then where are all of the other ponies?"

"There are quite a few in a pasture close by that still need some training, and the rest are out on the range. Remember when I told you part of a polo pony's training is to work cattle in the corral?"

"Yes."

"Good, because that is just a part of how they are trained. One of the most important aspects of a pony's training here in Argentina is to work them first at about one and a half years of age, for six or seven months on cattle out on the range. The gauchos do this as a part of their daily work routine. At the end of the six or seven months, the gauchos whose job it is to work these ponies will then evaluate their charges to see which ones are good enough to go on to the next step, which is working cattle in the corral. You see, not all ponies bred for polo make good polo ponies. Some just do not have what it takes."

"What if a pony can't make the grade? What happens to it then?" Jeff wanted to know.

"It is kept to be used to work cattle and sheep out on the range."

"Well, then if a pony makes it through the second part of its training, what comes next?"

"I was just getting to that. The ponies begin to play

what we call slow polo for one to one and a half months to see if they can adjust to playing polo. Not every horse can. This is the time, too, when we see if they can get along with other ponies. We look for things such as temperament, stamina, and smooth gallop, but this is probably the most important. If a pony cannot get along with the other ponies, it will be no good on the polo field. This is certainly not an in depth account of what it takes to train a pony, but may give you an idea."

"It really sounds like a lot of work goes into a pony's training. About how long," asked Jeff, "does it take to train a good polo pony?"

"A very good pony can be playing polo with a good polo team in two years. For a good-to-average pony, it talked about six months longer. We train our ponies here in Argentina faster than in most other countries. I think it takes about four years to train one in the United States."

Robert unlatched the top part of the door to the stall they had been standing in front of and swung it open. The horse inside immediately came to the door and stuck its head outside.

"He wants me to pet him," Robert said as the horse lowered its head so he could scratch behind its ears. "I call him Rabbit, because he is so fast and quick, and as you can see he does have rather long ears, which are almost like a rabbit."

"That is one beautiful animal," Jeff complimented, as he got into the act and began to scratch the horse on the neck.

As they stood, petting the horse, Jeff suddenly realized what Robert had said about this being his favorite polo pony, and asked him if he really played polo?

"Yes," Robert answered with a chuckle, "I do play polo, but there are a lot of polo players in Argentina. In fact, there are more than six thousand registered polo players in this country and most of them are very good."

"What do you mean, by very good? How do they rate a polo player anyway?"

"It may seem just a bit complicated, but really it's not, so I'll give you a quick rundown. A polo player is rated by the amount of goals he averages per game in one year. This is done each year. The very best players in the world are rated as ten-goal players."

"I guess a ten-goal player is kind of like a baseball player who gets to play in the All Star game, which is played only once a year. Only the best players in each of the two leagues are picked to play."

"I guess you could say that," Robert replied nodding his head. "About ninety percent of the world's ten-goal players are from Argentina."

"So, what you are telling me, is the ten-goal players are the very best?"

"Yes, but that does not mean they are the only good players. The goal or handicap system of ranking a player begins with minus two, then minus one, and then zero goals. From zero, it goes up to ten. Now, a player with a one or two rating is a good player. Players with a three or four goal rating are very good, so that should give you some kind of picture of how good a player is when compared to their rating."

"It seems to me," Jeff said, "like it could be kind

of unfair, though. Say a team had a couple of players who were really outstanding. One with an eight-goal and the other a ten-goal rating, while the other team only had a couple of players with a three-goal handicap. That hardly seems fair."

"Not to worry, because it doesn't work that way. Like you said, that would be rather unfair. Here's how it works. To make things more even, to make it simple, say the other two players on each team are not rated. The team with the total of the eighteen handicap has to give the team with the six-goal handicap, twelve goals before play begins. So, as you see, this does make things more even. Still, the team with the higher handicap would probably be favored to win the game. But that does not mean they would, though."

"About how long does it take to play a game of polo?"

"It can vary, depending on how many penalties there might be in a game," Robert answered. "But a game can consist of anywhere from four to eight chukkas. Here in Argentina, we play eight chukkas of six, at a half minute each. There is a break of four minutes between chukkas to change horses, because it is just too hard on the horse to play it more than one chukka. However, sometimes an exceptional horse will be played two chukkas, but usually it will be the first and last ones of the game. There is also a ten-minute break at half time. Each of the four players wears the number of their position on their jersey, which is one through four. Polo is a very team oriented game. Not only do the players have to work well together, but the horses, too. That is why it is so important to have good polo ponies. The horse can be the factor between winning and losing. But, to get to your original question, how long does it take to play a game of polo? As I said, it depends, but I would say an average game takes a little over one and a half hours."

"Is polo a very hard sport to learn to play?" questioned Jeff.

"That depends."

"Depends on what?"

"It depends on how hard a person is willing to work at it, and it, like other sports comes easier to some than it does to others."

"Did you have to work very hard to learn to play?"

"Yes, I had to work very hard, but I started at an early age and my hard work paid off."

"If you have one, what is your handicap?"

Yes, I do have a handicap. I am ranked as a five goal player, but only because I did work very hard, and still do."

"A five goal handicap at your age must mean you are a very good player."

"Now, you are embarrassing me, but yes, I guess you could say I am a good solid player."

"No, I didn't mean to embarrass you," apologized Jeff. "I was just trying to find out how good you are. One thing I was wondering, do polo players here in your country play for money?"

"No, here in Argentina polo is strictly an amateur sport. However, many of the top players do go to other countries to play and are very well paid. More often than not, in international play, the favored team is the one with the most Argentine players."

"I guess then, they must be among the best players in the world."

"Like I said before, Jeff, please don't think I'm bragging, but yes you are right. They are among the best, if not the best, in the world."

"Gee Robert, I don't think you're bragging at all. I would be proud of the fact. Anyway, show me some more. I would really like to see your whole layout."

"It's getting kind of late. You see, because we eat our evening meal around 9 o'clock, we always have something to eat in the late afternoon to get us through the evening until dinnertime. It's kind of like English teatime. But, we do have a little more time before we have to be back at the house, so I can show you around a little more."

They each gave Rabbit another good scratching and Robert closed the door. He showed Jeff through some of the other buildings. One was even a blacksmith's shop. This one was quite different from the one he had gotten to know so well in his friend Dorje's hidden village in far off Tibet. This one was big. They did everything from shoe horses to repair the estancia's machinery. There were neatly fenced corrals and pastures. Some held cattle or sheep while others held horses. On the way back to the house they passed a building Robert said was a clinic for the animals. A short way from the clinic was a row of covered bleachers. On the far side of the bleachers was the polo field.

"That's a pretty big field," Jeff said when Robert pointed it out to him. "Just how big is it anyway?"

"The field is three hundred yards long and two hundred yards wide."

"Wow, that's a lot bigger than an American football playing field."

Robert, checking his watch, said they had better head back to the house because by the time they got there, it would be time to eat, and they had better hurry because Nina did not like anyone to be late.

On the way, Robert suddenly snapped his fingers and said, "Jeff, I knew there was something I have been meaning to ask you, but I forgot."

"Ask away, Robert, ask away."

"Do you ride?"

"Do I ride? Do I ride what, buses? Trains? Bicycles? What kind of ride do you mean?" Jeff kidded.

"What I mean is, do you ride horses?" Robert quickly replied, and then realized Jeff had been kidding him, and they both laughed.

"As a matter of fact, I do ride horses," Jeff managed to answer when they had stopped laughing.

"That's great," Robert exclaimed. "I was afraid we might have to teach you, but we wouldn't mind. It's just that this is a very rugged country and an inexperienced rider could run into trouble."

They walked into the house just a minute or two late. When they got to the table, Nina faking a stern look, clucked her tongue and wagged her finger at Robert. Robert walked over to her, apologized for them being late. When he kissed her on the cheek, she broke into a warm smile and told them to sit down and eat.

After eating, Robert asked Jeff if he felt like taking a short ride?

"You bet," he said. "Just give me a couple of minutes to go up to my room to put on my western boots and I'll be ready."

Chapter 8

Jeff ran upstairs, found his boots in the closet, put them on and was back downstairs almost before Robert had realized he had gone. Glancing at Jeff's boots, Robert said they looked like they were made for riding horses.

"They are," Jeff answered. "These are the kind of boots used even today by cowboys in my country. The pointed toe makes it easy to slip the boots into the stirrups when you mount a horse and the kind of high heel is designed help keep the boot in the stirrup. Another of its uses is when a cowboy ropes an animal, like a calf, so it can be branded. When he jumps off his horse to tie the calf's legs together, you can dig the heels into the dirt, which gives him a lot more control over the calf. One thing they were not made for is walking. At least for any distance."

Back out at the stables, Robert asked Tomas if he would have a couple of the men go out to the corral and bring in a couple of horses so he and Jeff could take a ride. While they stood in the office waiting for

Tomas to return, Jeff happened to notice something he had missed earlier, an artist's easel standing in a corner and a table with several brushes and tubes of paints laying on its surface. "Who is the artist?" he asked with interest.

"Oh, Tomas is the artist I mentioned to you earlier. He is gaining quite a reputation here in Argentina. Actually, he only began to paint a few years ago when he couldn't work because he was sick. It gave him something to do. He's never even had a painting lesson. I guess he is just a natural artist. He paints mostly in watercolors, but several months ago a dealer in Buenos Aires suggested he try painting in oils as well, so he did. I really like his watercolors, but you know, his oils are really fantastic. Do you remember all of those paintings in the house? Not only in the gallery but in many of the other rooms?"

"Yes I do. I thought to myself that your house probably has more paintings hanging on its walls than most art galleries do."

"Many of those painting were done by famous artists throughout the world. Among them, you may have noticed, are several of Tomas' works. Of all of those paintings, I really like his paintings best of all.

"Tomas," cried Jeff. "I knew when you introduced him to me, the name seemed to ring a bell."

"What do you mean by ring a bell? I don't understand."

"It means his name sounded familiar, but I couldn't place in my mind why."

"I get it, that has happened to me, too. But why did his name ring a bell?"

"When we were in Buenos Aires, my dad bought a watercolor painting when we were shopping for gifts to send home. That painting was signed *Tomas*." I remember the salesperson said the scene was painted here in Patagonia by a gaucho whose talent was just being discovered. That painting must have been done by Tomas."

"Yes, I'm sure it probably was," replied Robert a little surprised. "He is a fine artist. But, Tomas is much more than that. He is like a second father to me. He is without a doubt one of the finest men I have ever known. Until he was injured, when he was much younger, he was a very fine polo player. He taught not only me, but also my father to play the game. He still advises my father about our ponies and coaches the estancia's polo team. Even though he can no longer play, he is still a very fine horseman, and participates in some of the traditional gaucho games that are played on horseback."

"I did notice he walked with a bad limp. Is the limp because of his injury?"

"Yes, his left leg was broken in several places as well as his hip."

"Was he playing polo when it happened?"

"No, it wasn't while he was playing polo. It happened when my father was only a small boy. My father, my grandfather, Tomas, and another gaucho who was actually an American, were riding after stray cattle high up in the canyon country. They were on a pretty narrow trail when an avalanche came thundering down the mountainside towards them. They were not able to turn around, and it was the American who made the others run for safety first while he brought up the rear."

"Did they all make it," Jeff asked rather anxiously.

"My father and my grandfather made it through, but just barely. Tomas, who was third in line, was caught by the very edge of the slide. His horse was killed and he was very badly injured. The American was not so fortunate, he did not make it and his body was never found. He was a very brave man. Another thing was the American actually saved my father's life two times. The first time was when his horse strayed into quicksand. The American gaucho just happened to hear his cries for help and was able to throw him a rope and pulled both my father and his horse to safety."

"Who was this American turned gaucho, anyway?" Jeff asked.

"From what I have been told," Robert began, "not much was ever known about him. It seems he just showed up one day asking for work and my grandfather hired him. I do know he was a very hard worker and quickly won the respect of my grandfather and the gauchos, something that does not come easily, because one must prove themselves—it must be earned. Everyone liked him and he seems to have been a well educated man. Tomas told these things to me. But, you must realize, people out here do not ask many questions of strangers. This is true in Patagonia, even today. If the person wants to tell anyone about themselves, well that is fine. But, if they do not, that is fine, too. A persons privacy is respected."

"I gather this American must have been quite a man?"

"Yes, from what I have been told, he was quite a man."

They could just hear the dull thud of horses hooves drawing closer, so they stepped out of the office just as Tomas and another gaucho came through the entrance to the barn. Each was leading a horse.

"How well do you ride?" Tomas asked Jeff.

"I think I'm a very good rider," he answered, trying not to sound as though he was patting himself on the back.

"I only ask, because our horses can be a bit spirited at times."

"Are these polo ponies or horses you use for cattle?" asked Jeff.

"No," replied Tomas, "these are not polo ponies, but they are very fine horses. Both have been used to work cattle and sheep. Now, the reason I asked how well you rode is because these horses are apt to be a little hard to handle and may act up at times so you keep that in mind and stay in control. If your horse gets to be a little feisty, remember to keep a very tight hold on the reins. But, I do not think you will have any problems, especially since you will be with Robert.

"Oh boy, thanks a lot Tomas," Robert kidded, giving Jeff a quick wink. "Now I guess it will be all my fault if Jeff has any trouble with his horse."

"These are very fine looking animals," Jeff said as he admired both horses.

The other gaucho handed Jeff the reins to his horse. As he was about to swing into the saddle, which was covered with a loose sheepskin, he asked where the saddle horn was?

"I'm used to riding with a western saddle that has a saddle horn to grab onto when you need it."

"Our Argentine saddles do not have saddle horns," Robert said. "But I'm sure you will get used to riding without one."

"Oh, I've ridden a lot with saddles without saddle horns when I was in Tibet. Lately, though, I've been riding using a western saddle, so I've kind got used to the old saddle horn again. But, like you said, I'll get used to riding without one."

Both Tomas and the other gaucho watched closely as Jeff swung into the saddle. They nodded to each other approvingly as he sat ready to follow Robert out onto the range.

Robert led the way through a maze of buildings and corrals. It wasn't long before they were out in open country. It only took Jeff a short time in the saddle to realize he was astride an exceptional horse and told Robert so.

Robert answered saying that both were very good horses.

"I know," he added. "Tomas told you these were not two of our polo ponies, but they were going to be."

"What do you mean, by going to be?"

"They are both offspring of our polo pony breeding program, but neither one quite made the grade. However, like I told you before, that does not mean they are not good horses to be used for cattle and sheep."

"How come they didn't make it?"

"Your horse did not seem to have the quickness it takes to make a good polo pony."

"What about the horse you're riding, what was his problem?"

"He does not seem to get along well with other horses, something a polo pony has to do."

"He seems to get along with my horse."

"Oh, with one or two and even three other horses he does fine. Any more than that and he tends to become a troublemaker. He has this habit of trying to boss other horses. He has even been known to bite them. I really don't ride him very often, but I guess Tomas thought it was time he was ridden. The horse I like to ride around like this has a sore hoof."

"Well, from what I've seen so far, you certainly do have a lot of horses to choose from."

"That is true," Robert said, "but even the gauchos, with their string of horses, usually have their favorite to ride, and so do I."

They were riding through an area of rolling grassland and seemed to be heading towards a long row of trees, behind which could be seen the outline of dull, colored, sandstone cliffs.

"Where are we headed, Robert. Any place special?"

"I thought we would take a short ride out to the river."

"Sounds good to me," answered Jeff. "How far is it?"

"It isn't far at all. Do you see that line of trees ahead, with those cliffs behind them?"

"Yes."

"The river runs just on the other side of the trees at the base of the cliffs. We'll be there in just a couple of minutes."

They circled around a small herd of cattle and several horses grazing on the lush grass. When they came near the horses, Robert really had to take control of his mount, because it really began to act up.

"I see what you mean about your horse not being able to get along with other horses," Jeff said when Roberts horse laid back its ears and tried to bite the nearest horse in the herd.

"He can be a real problem," Robert said, "but I was ready for what he might try and do. In every other way, though, he is an excellent animal."

It wasn't long before they entered the line of trees. On the other side they came out onto a grassy stretch on the banks of a small river.

"Wow, would you look at this!" exclaimed Jeff. "What a great looking stream. And clear, it's so clear it looks like I'm looking through a pane of window glass instead of water," he said, as he looked upstream and then downstream and back upstream with disbelief in his voice. "Robert, this looks like it could be the trout stream most trout fisherman only dreams of someday finding. Now, let me tell you, I have seen my share of trout streams in my rather young life," he added now feigning smugness in his voice, "but this stream, this little river, looks like it has just got to have trout in it. Yes, it's true I found streams in Tibet, streams full of trout. But the amount of time and effort involved to reach those streams is beyond the average persons comprehension. Never, even with my wild imagination, did I think I would ever see their equal, either in beauty or the quality of fish they held. I can truthfully say, as we sit here on these magnificent steeds that this stream, which runs right here before our very eyes, is as beautiful as any I have ever set eyes on. But now for the big question. Does it hold trout?"

"That was some speech and I, for one, am glad it's over," Robert kidded. "I take it you are a trout fisherman. However, to answer your question, yes, there are trout in this river. And even though I have never fished in Tibet, or in any other place but Scotland, when we would visit our relatives, I would be willing to bet this stream is as good as any trout stream you have ever fished."

"Am I a trout fisherman?" the young man answered. "Do birds fly? Do snakes crawl? Do dogs bark? I only eat and sleep to fly fish, especially for trout. But in all seriousness, I really do love to fly fish for trout. And by the way, do you trout fish?"

"You bet I do," answered Robert.

"Do you fly fish?"

"Again, you bet I do. I have already told you I play polo and I love the game. However, for me, even polo takes second place to fly fishing for trout."

Jeff became so excited when he heard how much Robert liked to fish and that he *fly-fished,* he almost fell off his horse. When he regained his balance he asked Robert if they could fish the river sometime.

His new friend told Jeff they could certainly fish the river whenever Jeff wanted. If he was too busy, Jeff could fish it by himself. The first time, however, they would fish it together.

He told Jeff the river was his anytime he wanted to fish it, but that there were several others on the estancia as well and though they all had trout in them, Robert felt this was his favorite.

"What about equipment?" Jeff said. "I didn't bring any with me."

"Equipment, don't worry because we have all of the stuff you will need. You see my grandfather was a very avid and skilled fly fisherman. He taught my father and in turn, my father taught me. My grandfather ordered almost all of his fly rods from a famous maker in your country and they are still as good today as when they were first made. I think we have over two-dozen rods and reels, as well as, all of the other equipment one needs. You see my grandfather was quite a collector of fly fishing equipment."

"What about trout flies? Do you have plenty of trout flies?"

"Yes, we do. My grandfather tied flies and we still fish with some he tied, but we order most of our flies from a dealer in the western part of your country, a fly fishing shop in the state of Montana."

"You said your grandfather tied his own flies? Do you or your father tie flies?"

"I guess my father did when he was a boy, but he hasn't tied since then. I've never learned, but I sure do wish I knew how. We still have all of my grandfathers fly tying tools and materials locked away in a cabinet."

"Well," Jeff said, "I tie flies. To me this really adds to the enjoyment I get out of fly-fishing. It's an added thrill to catch a trout on a fly you tied yourself. But, its very possible moths have eaten your grandfather's fly tying materials. Anyway, even if they have been, maybe we can salvage enough so that if you want, I can teach you the basics of how to tie flies."

"Would you really?"

"Of course. I do have to warn you that I am not the best teacher in the world."

"I could care less. Just teach me what you can. I remember once when I was about ten years old, I got out some of the feathers and other things and tried to tie a fly. What I came up with looked anything but a trout fly. It was so ugly I never tried to tie again. Anyway, we had better head back. By the time we clean up it should be time for dinner. If we have time tonight, I'll show you the fly tying materials and the other fishing stuff."

As they were about to turn their horses around and head back, Jeff happened to look at the ground. In the soft, damp sand at the very edge of the water he spied something that caused him to let out a cry as he pointed to a set of very large animal tracks of some kind. When he asked what they were, he was told they were the prints of a very large puma.

"The puma," Robert said, "is like the American mountain lion, but down here in Patagonia, they can grow much larger and this one, by the size of the tracks, is a giant. There are a lot of them in this area. See the cliff's on the far side of the river?"

"Yes."

"They are pock marked with caves of all shapes and sizes. Good places for a puma to live. The farther upstream you go, the wilder it gets."

"How far upstream do the cliffs go?" Jeff asked.

"They go for miles and miles. It seems the farther you go, the more caves there are. We've lost a few sheep to pumas in the last month or so and a couple of cows. Normally, they leave the cows alone because they are too big for the average puma to bring down. Sometimes they will kill a calf, but by the size of those tracks this puma is certainly big enough to bring down a fully grown cow. These are the same tracks some of the gauchos have seen. I can tell because it is missing a toe on its left front paw. Gauchos tend to be very superstitious."

"What does that have to do with it?" Jeff wanted to know.

"Oh, there is talk among them."

"What do you mean by talk among them?"

"Some of them seem to think this particular cat is a phantom or ghost. Not living."

"What makes them think that? It sounds kind of spooky."

"More than once a gaucho has come upon a newly killed sheep. And, more than once, because of the open country where it happened, the gaucho should have been able to see the puma. No one has ever seen it. All they have seen are its tracks and they just seem to melt into the earth when they try and follow them. It is the same animal because one of its toes is missing on its left front paw. The way they talk, the animal just seems to be able to vanish and reappear at will or maybe even change into another form of animal whenever it wants too."

As they rode slowly away from the riverside, they were not able to see their every move was being watched by a pair of yellow eyes from high above, near the top of the cliff on the far side of the river.

"Now, it sounds even more spooky," Jeff said, referring to Roberts last statement. "I'm not superstitious, but it certainly isn't for me to say whether this can happen or not. How big do you think this cat really is, anyway?"

"Those tracks are probably twice as big as the average size puma tracks."

"Oh, boy, this might be some kind of world record or something. I can understand why someone's imagination might be captured by those tracks. But you said the cat has never been seen. That probably adds a lot to the story. Are all gauchos superstitious?"

"I think so. Some, of course may be more so than others. As an example, a couple of weeks before you arrived, Tomas came to my father and told him a strange gaucho had just rode in asking for a job."

"What is so odd about that?"

"Nothing, really. Gauchos tend to be nomadic and independent. Often they work until they earn some money and will then move on. I think those gauchos who work here on our estancia are the exception. Many have been working here all of their working lives. Some were born on the estancia."

"Where do all of these gauchos live? I know I've just arrived, but I haven't seen any gauchos other than the ones we had maté with in Tomas' office. What about their wives and kids?"

"Those who are married and have children are housed on one of the other headquarters of the estancia. This headquarters also has a school. Because we are so far from the nearest school my grandfather had one built here on the estancia. That is the place he decided to build the school."

"How many kids go to this school, anyway?"

"There are, on the average, around twenty five, some years less, some years more. There are two teachers and the children get a very good basic education. Some of the single gauchos, and even some with wives, but with no school aged children, prefer to live in one of the many small houses scattered out on the estancia. If a married gaucho's wife who lives in one of these houses has a baby, when the baby is old enough to attend school, they will then move into a house near the school."

"Does this system really work? I meant it sounds kind of like they are left to do their own thing."

"In a way they are," Robert said. "However, they each have their responsibilities. They know what their job is and what they have to do. Believe me, they really are hard and trusted workers."

They were almost back to the horse barn when Jeff reminded Robert he had started to tell him about the gaucho Tomas had gone to his father about.

"I'm glad you reminded me," Robert said tapping the side of his head with a finger, "because I had forgotten all about it. Anyway, this man asked for work. My father told Tomas whatever he wanted to do was fine with him. Normally, you see, Tomas would not even have asked my father. He is entrusted to make his own decisions, but this time he felt he should go to my father. He felt there was just something not quite right with the man and he thought my father should talk to him. As a favor, my father agreed."

"What was the problem? Was he some kind of a nut or something?"

"I can't say, but Tomas said the man has an evil eye."

"I don't understand. What did he mean by that? Just what is an evil eye?"

"One of his eyes has a film over it. I guess he was probably born that way. My father talked to the gaucho and even though he was not totally at ease about hiring him, he knew he needed work, so he gave Tomas the okay."

"Did he work out? Is he still working here on the ranch?"

"Yes, he is working here, but Tomas is really keeping a close watch on him. He put him to work around the stables just as a trial. According to Tomas, the man seems to be doing his job, but does grumble a lot about what he has to do and seems to have a really bad temper. The other gaucho's tend to stay clear of him. They are instinctive about things. Of course, nothing is known about his background, because here in Patagonia, we don't ask about such things. Like I said, Tomas is keeping a close watch on him."

They were just coming around the corner of the stables when the quiet of the evening was broken by the sound of high-pitched screaming and yelling. They each jumped off their horse and ran towards the office where the sounds seemed to be coming from. What they saw when they entered the office made each of their mouths drop open in astonishment. Two gauchos were holding a third by his arms. The one being held was doing the screaming, along with a lot of kicking and threatening, and trying his best to get at Tomas, who stood as calmly as the situation would allow behind his desk. When Jeff and Robert walked in, the room fell suddenly quiet. The gaucho stopped his struggling, but kept a defiant one-eyed glare pointed at Tomas.

"What is going on here?" Robert asked in a puzzled voice.

"I caught this man, "Tomas began in a cool voice, "mistreating one of the horses. That, as you know, is something I will not stand for."

"And, rightly so," Robert agreed.

"As a result of this incident I have told him he is to leave the estancia, immediately. He began to argue. When he saw I meant what I said, he became violent and threatened me. As you can see, I was not alone and when he lunged at me, well, it was fortunate Carlos and Alex were close enough to grab him before any harm was done," Tomas said pointing to the two gauchos who held the man.

The gaucho, whose flint sharp features and menacing smile were made even more menacing by the evil look in his one good eye, finally spoke.

"Miguel, my name is Miguel," he said through clinched teeth, as he stared straight at Robert.

"Well, Miguel," Robert said staring right back at the gaucho, "if Tomas said you are through, well then, you are through and had better leave."

The gaucho shook loose, turned, spat on the floor, and walked quickly out into the barn. Tomas said the man's horse was saddled just outside, but the gaucho went over to a ladder leaning against the wall, picked it up, swung it around his head and smashed it against the edge of a heavy beam causing it to break in half. He began to behave like a madman. He threw the piece he still had in his hands onto the floor and began to jump up and down on it until it was nothing more than shattered pieces. When he was through, he turned toward the astonished group, shook his fist, yelled they would pay for what they had done to him, turned, walked quickly outside, mounted his horse and spurred it into a dead run in the direction of the distant mountains.

"Well, Tomas," Robert said as they walked back into the office, "I guess you were right about that man. There certainly is something wrong with him."

It was at that point, Jeff noticed a large knife lying on the floor. "Whom does this belong to?" he asked as he picked it up and handed it to Tomas.

"It belongs to Miguel," Alex said. "He pulled the knife on Tomas, just before Carlos and myself were able to get to him. It took some doing, but we were finally able to wrestle it away from him."

"Good work, the both of you. It is just too bad this had to happen, but better now than later on," Robert said with the others agreeing.

The little group, Jeff included, felt a sense of relief now that the troublemaking gaucho was gone. What they did not, and could not have known, was they had not seen the last of the gaucho with the evil eye.

Chapter 9

They timed it just right. After cleaning up they met
back downstairs. This time they even had a couple of
minutes to spare before dinner was served. When they
did sit down, Robert asked Nina, why there were only
enough places set for the three of them.

"Your father," she said with a sigh, "and Mr. Thornton, decided to spend the night instead of coming back
here. They may be there for a few days, but he will let
me know for certain tomorrow. He said for you to take
good care of Jeff, and for the both of you to stay out of
mischief."

Nina's last words caused Robert's face to break out
in a large grin.

After eating, Jeff felt so full he did not think he
would be able to get up from the table—that is until
Robert asked if he was too tired to have a look at the fly
tying materials and the fishing equipment.

"Are you kidding," came Jeff's quick response. He
had been sitting slouched down in his chair, but sat

upright when Robert had asked the question. After excusing themselves from the table, Robert led the way.

As they were walking out of the dining room, Jeff heard Nina mutter good-naturedly, "Fishing and polo, how this family loves their fishing and polo. Sometimes I think Robert would rather even fish than eat."

At the back of the house, Jeff was taken down a long hall. At the end was a large, closed, heavy wooden door. After opening the door, Robert motioned for Jeff to enter the room.

"This," Robert said as he turned on a light, "is what we call our game room."

Jeff stood motionless. Only his head and eyes moved. His mouth hung open. For once in his life he was almost speechless. The room was like something you only read about in books or saw in movies.

Along the right hand wall, which was closest to the door, were several rows of shelves. Lining the shelves were polo trophies of all sizes and shapes. Photographs of polo being played, polo ponies with smiling players mounted on them in singles and group shots hung on the same wall. A large, stone fireplace protruded from the center of the wall at the far end of the spacious room. On each side of the fireplace were shelves of books. Robert told Jeff the books were about polo and fly-fishing. Many, he said, were very old and quite rare. In front of the fireplace, was a low table. On one side of the table was a long leather couch. Scattered on the other side were three matching leather chairs. Over the fireplace hung a painting of a fly fisherman knee-deep in a trout stream, casting to an unseen fish. Jeff now turned his gaze towards the left hand wall. A glass-fronted cabinet took more than half of this wall up. Lining the back of the cabinet was a long row of standing metal fly rod cases in various lengths. Keeping good company with the fly rods were at least two-dozen or more English-made fly reels. Each was placed on its own miniature shelf. The rest of the wall was taken up by a window at the end of which was a door Robert said was the entrance they used when they came in from fishing. Just outside was a row of pegs to hang wet waders and hip boots so they could dry. They were now walking around the room. As Jeff explored with Robert at his side, a thick carpet muffled the sound of their footsteps. Near the fireplace, Jeff turned to look back at the door he had entered. The door was set almost in the very corner. A few feet out from the wall was a good-sized table with six chairs around it. The back of this wall was taken up by another set of cabinets. These, though, were all wood. Jeff asked what was in them. Robert said this was where they stored their hip boots, waders, fly-fishing vests, flies and anything else having to do with fly-fishing. "But, come over here," he said leading Jeff by the arm to two rows of drawers at the end of the cabinet. "In these drawers is where all of the fly tying materials are kept."

Robert began to pull open deep drawers, while Jeff, eagerly checked out their contents. Each one housed the various kinds of feathers, furs, hooks and the other kinds of things used in fly tying. The strong, but pleasant smell of cedar wood began to fill the air.

"Wow," Jeff exclaimed, "that smell of cedar is really strong."

"Yes it is. My grandfather had all of the drawers and the rest of this cabinet lined with cedar wood."

"Your grandfather sure knew what he was doing," Jeff said as he continued checking out the drawers, "because I don't see any kind of damage at all to this stuff. There certainly haven't been any moths in any of these drawers. So far, everything looks like it's in great condition."

"Why would that be? Those materials have been in there for years. You would think at least one moth would have found it."

"It's because your grandfather knew what he was doing."

"What do you mean by that?" Robert asked.

"There are two sure-fire ways of preventing moths from getting into and devouring things like these feathers," Jeff said as he showed Robert some nice feathers from the neck of a rooster. "Now, I don't know just how much you know about how to preserve your flies and fly tying materials, but these rooster neck feathers are of a very high quality. The quality used only to tie the very best dry flies. Actually, in fly tying jargon, this is referred to as a rooster neck or cape. And, as you might have guessed, it comes from the neck of a rooster. As you can see, the feathers are still attached to the roosters' skin. See how stiff and shiny the barbs of the feathers or hackles, as we call them, are?"

"Yes, I see what you mean, but what about the cedar? What does that have to do with anything?"

"Like I was saying, there are two ways to make sure moths won't eat this stuff. There may be other ways, but the two I know about are mothballs and cedar wood. The drawback with mothballs is that they need replenishing every so often, but cedar does not. The smell of cedar wood never goes away. It lasts as long as the wood and I guess it must be the smell that does the job. Your grandfather had to have known what he was doing because he had the rest of the cabinet lined with cedar as well. Moths have been known to eat everything, but the hook on flies. How would you like to get to the stream, open your fly box and find nothing but bare hooks? Not a good thought."

"What would have happened if my grandfather had not done this?"

"My guess," Jeff replied, "is when we opened these drawers tonight, instead of finding everything in good shape we would have found nothing but a lot of dust. What a huge letdown that would have been."

"Does it look like there are enough of the kinds of materials you would need to tie flies?"

Jeff, still checking through the drawers, said it looked to him like there was enough of everything to tie thousands of flies.

"What do you mean by everything?"

"To begin with," began Jeff. "In this top drawer, we have all kinds of rooster necks of the colors needed to tie just about any pattern of dry fly ever invented. Also there are plenty of the softer necks that come from hens, not roosters, but hens, to tie wet flies and nymphs. Now, look at this next drawer. It's full of all kinds of different kinds of fur."

"What do you use fur for?"

"Mostly, to make the body of a fly. I'll teach you how to do that when I teach you to tie. And, certain kinds of fur are used to imitate the wings of some patterns of flies. It has other uses too, but I won't get into that just now."

Jeff went on opening drawers and explaining about the various uses of the materials found in each. One drawer contained boxes and boxes of fly tying hooks in all sizes. Another, held spools of fly tying threads and spools of various colored silk called floss, which is used to make bodies on certain flies. A very specially designed drawer held all the tools necessary to tie flies. Each tool was placed in its own place. Each drawer seemed to hold treasure. Jeff told Robert he felt he had discovered the mother lode."

"What do you mean by *mother lode?* I don't understand," Robert said in a puzzled voice.

"To discover the mother lode means to strike it rich. Like, for instance, if you were prospecting for gold and you found it, lots of it, then you found the mother lode. It's not only this fly tying stuff; it's all of these rods and reels, too. You don't have to find gold, it can be things just like this."

"I get it," Robert beamed. "It doesn't really have to be a real treasure, one worth millions of dollars. It depends on the value something has for an individual, like all of these fly tying materials and fly-fishing equipment. This is a real treasure for you, because you love to fly fish and tie your own flies."

"Exactly. Now, how about having a look at some of this other stuff?"

"Sure, feel free to look at anything you want."

After looking through the other parts of the cabinet and commenting on the fact there was enough equipment stored away to start a sporting goods store, Jeff said, "Now, I guess its time to have a look at the fly rods and reels."

After taking several rods out of their cases, Jeff, said, "I just can't believe what you have here, Robert. Do you know anything at all about bamboo fly rods?"

"No, not really. My grandfather bought them a long time ago. My father sent to America several years ago for a new rod for each of us. The new rods are made from graphite, not bamboo like these here. Are these rods any good? Are they still in good enough shape to be fished?"

"Let me explain something to you, but stop me if you already know what I am going to say. Graphite rods are the newest material used in rod making. It is lighter than bamboo. The bamboo rods you have, here were all made by a very famous maker of bamboo rods in the United States. I am no expert on bamboo rods, but because I use one myself, and really like them, I have done a lot of research. The rod I use at home is not the quality of your rods. The man who made these rods has been dead for many years now. His rods are prized by anyone lucky enough to own one, and you have over two dozen of his rods," Jeff said with envy in his voice. "They all seem to have been very well cared for. I found only one with a problem and that is minor."

"If they are in such good condition, does that mean they can be used? Or, should they be left alone and not fished at all?"

"Let me put it this way, Robert. When a bamboo rod is built, and let me add something here real quick, it takes a very highly skilled person a lot of hours to build a really fine one, and when that rod is finished, it should be fished with. They are great rods to fish with and it would really be a shame if you did not fish these or at least some of them. They were made to be fished. You know, the thing that sets bamboo apart from other materials they make rods from? No two are exactly alike. Each one is different. For example, they can make graphite rods so that each one can be just the same as the next. Say a company builds a certain model of graphite rod in a certain weight, length, and action. They may make hundreds or thousands of that model and each will be exactly the same. Don't get me wrong, that is what most people who fly fish want. There are still those of us who love to fish and really appreciate bamboo rods. One of the reasons, I think is because no two will ever be exactly alike."

"Why."

"To make a long story short, bamboo is a product of nature, not man. It is a living plant whereas, graphite and glass, the other materials used, are man-made. This is what sets bamboo apart, the fact it is a natural material. No two, bamboo rods are ever exactly the same. Each one will be different. The rod maker may try to build two to be exactly the same, but the expert can tell the difference. I think what I am trying to say is bamboo rods, because they are never the same, tend to have a personality, where rods made from other materials do not. Bamboo rods tend to become like a friend. They have warmth about them. Graphite and glass seem to be cold, unfriendly. Bamboo is just the opposite. Maybe, this all sounds a little far fetched, but those who fish bamboo rods would know what I am trying to say."

"I think I get it," Robert said, "when you say bamboo rods have a personality. Do you know what...I think I will start fishing with bamboo rods. I used to before we got our graphite rods, but I really did not understand or know anything about them."

Jeff had a quick look at the fine quality made English fly reels, when all of a sudden he realized how tired he was, and told Robert so. Robert answered saying it had been a long day for each of them, but much longer for Jeff.

"Tomorrow," he added, "you can sleep late. I'll wake you and if you feel up to it, we could go fishing. It just happens to be the opening day of our trout season."

"That sounds good to me," came Jeff's sleepy, but still enthusiastic reply. "I think I'll sleep good tonight."

Jeff could not know, but he was about to have a very strange experience.

Chapter 10

Jeff's eyelids felt like lead curtains as he crawled into bed. Sleep came almost before his head hit the pillow.

It was sometime during the night when the almost always-present Patagonian wind began to blow harder. Jeff, even being as exhausted as he was, was still a light sleeper. He woke with a start when an extra hard gush of wind blew open the doors leading out onto his balcony. Bleary eyed, he forced himself to get out of bed to go close them. On the way, he stubbed a toe on his boots. The shock of the pain caused him to become at least partially awake. Now hopping on his good foot, he reached the doors, and had to fight another gush of wind to close them. It wasn't until he had limped half way back to bed that he realized he thought he had seen someone out on the balcony staring in at him. He turned and looked back. Now, all he could see was the bright silver light only a full moon can create. Back in bed, his last thoughts, before sleep again overtook him, were of the mysterious figure, and how as he struggled to close the doors. It just seemed to fade away into nothingness.

The next morning at breakfast when Robert asked him how he slept, Jeff kind of off-handedly mentioned what he thought he had seen, and Robert quickly changed the subject. Jeff, thought he might try and bring it up again before breakfast was over, but quickly forgot when Robert said it looked like a fine day outside; the kind of day a person should spend on the banks of a trout stream. Jeff, of course, was in total agreement and said so. Robert said they had better finish their breakfast so they could get their equipment together and be on their way. Jeff, who was now on his second helping, still had plenty of food on his plate. It seemed to disappear in record time.

Standing by the cabinet in the game room, Robert asked Jeff what size shoe he wore. When Jeff told him, Robert opened a door where several pair of hip boots and chest high fishing waders were hanging in a row.

"Here, take these," Robert said handing Jeff a pair of rubber-hip boots. "They are just your size." After taking a pair for himself, he opened another part of the cabinet, the part where the fishing vests were kept. Again, there were several hanging from individual pegs. Each vest, Robert said held the necessary things all fly fishers need on the stream; leaders, extra leader material, clippers to cut the leader material, dry fly dressing to put on a dry fly so it will float better, and just about anything else he would need.

"What about the flies? I don't see any fly boxes in this vest," Jeff said.

"Ah yes, flies. As you know, these drawers over here

are where the flies are kept. Here are two boxes for you to use. As you can see, one holds dry flies in various patterns and sizes, and the other wet flies, nymphs and a few large streamer flies. Those big streamers will sometimes take big fish. Most of the patterns in both boxes seem to work well on our streams. But, you probably know as well as me, trout can be very picky when it comes to what fly they will take."

"Thanks," Jeff said as he placed the boxes in a pocket of his vest, "and by the way," he added, "where are we going to fish today?"

"I thought we would ride out again and fish near where I took you to see the river yesterday. I think we will go a little farther upstream, though. How does that sound to you?"

"That sounds great. From what you showed me yesterday, you couldn't ask for a prettier or fishier looking stream. But now what about a rod and reel?"

"The best for last," Robert replied with a smile. "I'll let you choose the rod you want to use."

After checking out several rods, Jeff finally picked a three-piece rod, eight feet long. "Judging by the size of the river we are going to fish," Jeff stated, "this is probably as good a rod as any here."

"A good choice, I think," Robert said as he handed Jeff the matching reel for the rod. "I will not be using my graphite rod. I want to start fishing with bamboo rods like I told you last night. Do you have any suggestions?"

"I think so," Jeff answered, "Why don't you use another eight foot rod. I think this one right here would have been my other choice. I don't really know why I chose the one I did, instead of that one. They are both eight feet long and are three pieces. The action of the rods is similar, but anyway, I chose this one. But they both feel really good to me. And it seems to me, a three piece, rather than a two piece rod would be a little easier to carry on horseback."

"I will gladly take your advice and use this rod. Now, I guess we have everything we will need, but we do have to stop by the kitchen and pick up our lunch to take with us."

After a quick trip to the kitchen, where Nina, handed each of them a lunch, and told them to have a good time, but to be careful, they headed for the horse barn.

Tomas wasn't in his office, but they found him just outside, checking the horse that had been abused by the gaucho with the evil eye.

"How is the horse doing," Robert asked.

"Oh, I think he is doing fine," answered Tomas, "He is still a little bit nervous when I approach him, but he is getting better and it seems like I am gaining his trust."

"As you can probably tell," whispered Robert, "Tomas not only loves horses, but has a way with them. But then, they seem to love him just as much. I have seen him train even the most stubborn horse to ride. So stubborn and hard to handle, even the other gauchos could not train it. Usually the horse ends up following Tomas around just like a dog would. Yes, Tomas is what you might call a very rare human being."

"I think this is enough for today," Tomas said as he

patted the horse on the neck. "Let me put him in a stall. I will be back shortly with your horses."

It wasn't long before Tomas came back leading their horses. He handed each a lead rope, and said because all of the gauchos were out working, he had things to do and he would let them saddle their own horses.

"Can you saddle a horse, Jeff?" Robert asked.

"Well, sure, I think I can handle it, okay."

The incident of what happened to him the time he and Trudy were saddling the horses back home flashed into Jeff's brain. He vowed he would not make the same mistake twice. He would make extra sure this horse did not hold its breath in when he cinched up the saddle.

After tying the horses to a post, Robert led the way to the tack room. When he opened the door, they were greeted by the rich smell of well cared for leather. Around the walls was a row of saddles, each placed on a kind of wooden frame. Hanging on the walls behind the saddles were the bridles.

"Would you look at all of those saddles and bridles? I have never seen so many in my life," Jeff said almost under his breath. "Everything looks so well cared for and neat. And, that smell of polished leather...isn't it great."

"This is the tack room where Tomas keeps the equipment for the working horses, and like you, Jeff, I really like the smell of this place. I have polished every piece of equipment in this room more times than I can count. It became my job when I was eight years old. It's very hard work, but you know something, I loved doing it."

"Do you still do it? Do you still polish all of this leather?"

"No, not any more. It was my job for many years, though and if I didn't do a good job on a saddle, Tomas would make me do it over again. Yes, polishing these saddles taught me a lot."

"You said this was the tack for the working horses on the estancia. Do you mean to tell me you have another tack room? And if you do, what is that equipment for?"

"We do have another tack room. The equipment kept there is what is used for polo. Someday, I'll show it to you but not today. Today, we are going trout fishing."

Robert then pointed to a saddle and bridle, telling Jeff they were his and to go ahead and get them while he got another. The saddle and bridle, as well as, the horse, were the same as he had used yesterday, and would be his to use any time he wanted while he was staying at the estancia. Robert also told him it was a sign of trust for Tomas to let Jeff go ahead and saddle his own horse. Tomas usually did this or he would have one of the other gauchos do it when a guest staying at the estancia wanted to ride. You see one has to prove to Tomas they know how to handle a horse."

When Robert told this to Jeff, a feeling of humbleness spread through his body. He felt humble because a man of Tomas' obvious importance and standards had granted him this trust, and this from a man he had met only the day before.

I guess, Jeff thought to himself, I must have made a good impression on this man.

Jeff saddled and bridled his horse without any problems. He did, however, make extra certain the cinch was adjusted just right.

They had just finished tying their equipment onto the back of their saddles when Robert said, "How stupid can I get? I knew there was something I forgot to get."

"What do you mean?" Jeff asked.

"Hold on just a minute and I'll show you," Robert answered as he ran back into the tack room. He came running back shortly holding two long, rather wide, adjustable leather straps.

"What are those?" Jeff questioned.

"Here, you take this one and I'll show you. Tomas made several of these. As you can see there are two short straps about two feet apart, each with a buckle, sewn to the wide strap. What you do is, place one of the short straps around one end of your rod case and tighten it and the other around the other end. Now, what you have is a sling, kind of like a rifle sling. You put it over your shoulder like this so the case hangs across your back at an angle. This way the case won't be hanging on the saddle and getting in your way."

"What a great idea," Jeff said as he buckled the straps around his rod case and slung it over his shoulder. "You hardly even know it's there."

They mounted their horses and Robert led the way out onto the open range. Jeff wondered if Robert felt as excited as he did. Here he was in a strange, and beautiful country, with a new friend, and they were going trout fishing on a river he had never before fished. He had reason to be excited. In fact, he was so excited he couldn't hold back anymore and let out a loud yell that caused the horses to prance around to show they were excited, too. Robert laughed and at the top of his voice, said he had the feeling it was going to be a fantastic day.

Chapter 11

The first part of the ride took them on the same trail as yesterday. They were talking, kidding back and forth about who was going to catch the biggest or the most fish, when Robert veered off to the left in the direction of the mountains.

"Is where we are going much farther than where we went yesterday?" Jeff asked.

"No, it really isn't much farther at all. The pools where I am going to take you hold some very big trout."

"Do these fish ever feed on the surface or do we have to fish for them down deep with big nymphs or wet flies of some kind?"

"Oh, they feed on the surface. They will often take a big, bushy dry fly if there are no insects hatching. If there is a hatch of insects today the fish can get very picky."

"You mean you had better have a good imitation of

the insect hatching or your chances of getting any fish are pretty slim?"

"You got it," replied Robert matter-of-factly.

"What kind of insects do you have down here? Do you have the same as we have in my country, like mayflies, and caddis flies?"

"Yes, we do," Robert said, "we have several species of mayflies, caddis flies, and we also have a freshwater crab in our rivers the fish really go for, and it really makes them grow and put on weight quite fast. However," added Robert, "most of the fishing on our streams here on the estancia is done with the dry fly."

"That's great, because dry fly fishing is my favorite way to fish. I like wet fly and nymph fishing, but there is nothing quite like the thrill you can get when a nice trout takes your dry fly."

"I agree," Robert said shaking his head in agreement, "that is a special thrill only a fly fisherman experiences."

They rode in silence for several minutes through an area of sagebrush and stubby yellow grass. As they were just topping a slight rise not far from the river, Jeff glanced off to one side and let out a yelp of surprise and hollered, pointing, "What the heck is that thing? Man can it run. It looks like some kind of ostrich."

"That's a rhea," laughed Robert. "It's related to the African ostrich, but it's smaller, and you bet it really can run. That one is probably a big male. There is a good chance his harem of females is around here somewhere. The gauchos hunt them with bolas."

"You mean one of those things they swing around their heads and throw?"

"That's what I mean."

"Tell me, Robert, what actually is a bola, anyway?" Jeff wanted to know.

"A bola," Robert began, "is made of three fairly long woven leather thongs. At the end of each thong, is attached a leather covered lead ball. One of the balls is held in the hand while the person using the bola whirls the other two around his head. When the person let's go of the bola it travels at a very high rate of speed towards its target. They can just as easily entangle the legs of a wild, range steer as they can a fast running rhea. It's amazing what a gaucho can do with his bola, they are so expert at using them."

"I can believe it, because you would really have to be an expert to bring down one of those two legged speedsters."

They were getting pretty close to the river. On the far side, the tilted walls of the cliffs rose high above them. Jeff really had to bring his head way back to see the top.

They halted on a grassy knoll at the river's edge. Here, the sweeping current formed a long, trouty-looking pool before tumbling into a series of short, boulder-strewn rapids. Upstream, the bank on their side of the river was park-like with ankle-high grass growing to within a few feet of the water's edge. There were just enough trees and scattered bushes to offer areas of shade when needed from the hot sun. They found an especially grassy and shady spot near a large, flat rock to tie the horses. Before getting off his horse, Jeff glanced upstream where he could see a huge bank of dark cumulus clouds piling up over the top of the mountain peaks. "Do you think it will rain on us today?" he asked Robert, as he pointed towards the clouds.

"No, those clouds will probably not reach us until sometime tonight," came Robert's positive answer.

It was warm and pleasant by the river. Every once in a while the breeze would stiffen causing the leaves in the trees to dance and twirl in a jig.

"This, is a perfect day for fishing," cried Jeff happily as they sat on the edge of the flat rock putting on their hip boots. "I can't think of any place on earth I would rather be right now than here getting ready to go fishing in this beautiful river."

"I'm glad you feel that way, because do you know something?" came Roberts smiling reply, "I could not agree with you more. It is a beautiful day. It is a beautiful river. Even if we do not catch a single trout, it will still be a wonderful day."

"You said it, my friend, you said it."

"There is something I have been meaning to tell you."

"What is it?" Jeff asked.

"Well, let's suppose you were out riding by yourself and you had an accident."

"Have an accident, what do you mean?" Jeff asked frowning.

"Say for instance, for some reason you fell off your horse or twisted your ankle while fishing and couldn't get to your horse...what would you do?"

"I don't know. I really never thought about it."

"As you can see this is a very wild and desolate country. So, if you ever do get into any kind of trouble, the signal for help is to light a bush on fire. The smoke rising from the fire is a distress signal. It means some one is in trouble and needs help. Anyone who sees the smoke will come to your aid. Do you carry any matches with you?"

"No. Never. At least not unless I'm going camping." Jeff answered.

"Here, take these, and never, never ride out anywhere without them," Robert said seriously, as he handed Jeff a small waterproof container filled with matches. "I don't want to sound dramatic or anything," he added, "but you never know what might happen out here. There may be a time when they will come in handy. They may even save your life. I hope such a time will never come, but it is certainly better to have them just in case."

"Thanks, Robert. I will always keep them in my pocket. I'm glad they're in a waterproof container, though."

"Why is that?"

"As Trudy Garrison, my best friend back home, would gladly tell you if she were here with us, I seem to have a habit of falling in when I'm fishing. I don't do it every time I'm on the stream, but I do it enough for her to have given me the title of World Champion Faller Inner. Anyway, I have to admit, I do seem to fall in quite a lot."

Finally, their hip boots were on, rods were assembled and they were ready to go fishing.

"I thought we might begin near the head of this long pool," Robert said, "At this time of day, the fish seem to be along the far bank, from where the current enters the pool down to where it tapers off. In the evening, they can be all over the pool when they feed."

"Robert, I am in your hands. Do you have any suggestions about what pattern of fly I should tie on?" Jeff replied.

"I think so. It looks like there aren't any insects hatching out," Robert said as he scanned the surface of the pool. "Let's see what you have in your box of dry flies."

After checking through Jeff's box of flies, Robert, finally chose a large brown hackled fly with a red body and white calf tail wings. "This fly," he told Jeff, "is usually a good fly to use when there are no trout rising to insects on the surface. As you can see, it's big and fluffy. I guess a trout sees it as a pretty big mouthful, so worth the effort to come up to the surface for."

"That looks like a good fly to me," Jeff said as he tied the fly onto his leader. "What are you going to start out with, Robert?"

"Actually, I think I'll use the same pattern, only one with a green body instead of a red body, like the one you are going to use. That way we can see if the trout prefer one over the other."

"Good thinking, my friend, good thinking."

Robert led the way upstream along the faint trail and stopped on a low rise just at the edge of the river, across from the bottom of the current. They just stood there for a minute taking it all in. The water looked to be in perfect condition. The only sound they heard was the cry of an angry bird and the murmur of the river. Again, but this time to himself, Jeff thought there was nowhere he would rather be than standing right where he was. The only thing missing was Trudy. He knew she would feel exactly the same if she were standing there instead of him. Their silence was broken when Robert, pointing his rod, told Jeff where to cross and begin his casting.

"Robert, I think I see where you mean. Over on the far side where the current slows and looks a little deeper? Begin there and work upstream. Is that where you mean?"

"Yes, and it's easy to wade far enough across so you can work your way into a good casting position without any problem. There are usually some nice trout lined up all along the far bank. Not only is it a good place for them to live, but the current is probably just fast enough so it brings them a lot of food, too. I'll stand here, and if you need it I can kind of guide you across from here."

"No, you go first," insisted Jeff.

"You are my guest," Robert answered politely, "I would not be a very good host if I was to go first."

"If you put it that way, I'll give it a try first."

Jeff walked to the edge and entered the river. He began working his way up at Robert's suggestion, so he would be a little below where the current on the far side slowed down. The river's bottom was solid and not slippery, so it was easy wading. Only once did Jeff falter, when the toe of his boot struck against a rock causing him to lose his balance, but only for a second.

"Hey, clumsy," he muttered angrily, "watch where you're going. Boy, I would really feel stupid if I fell in right here in front of Robert." Now, watching his step, Jeff worked his way into what he felt was a good casting position, and yelled to Robert, "what do you think, does this look about the right place to begin casting?"

"You might edge your way just a few more feet downstream and a little closer to the far bank," answered Robert. "It may not look like it, but there are some real tricky currents and you really have to be in the right spot or they will cause your fly to drag almost as soon as it hits the water. That usually won't happen though, for you will tend to get a natural float when you are closer to the bank."

Jeff did as Robert directed. As he stood studying the water, he could see what Robert had meant. There were some real tricky currents he had not noticed before. Unless he were in exactly the right casting position, this was the kind of stretch of water that could give a fly fisherman nightmares.

Having worked his way into position and studied the situation, Jeff began to lengthen out line to make his first cast. Now, the only sounds were the soft murmur of the current and the switching sound made by the back and forth motion of his fly rod as Jeff made his first cast. The fly landed rather heavily on the water but began to float back downstream towards him, just like it was a natural insect. Nothing happened. Not then or for several casts. Jeff worked his way slowly upstream, casting, letting the fly drift down with the glistening, foam-flecked current of the river. It was near the top of the pool when it happened. He had just made a cast where the fly landed tight up against the bank. It was a part of the bank the current had caused to become deeply undercut, the near perfect spot for a big trout. The current swung against the bank creating a slow whirlpool. This, Jeff told himself, would be the last cast for this fly. If a fish did not take it on this cast he was going to change to another pattern. The fly landed in the middle and began to follow the circular motion of the whirlpool. The trout just seemed to materialize out of nowhere. Its huge form just drifted up casually from the clear depths. The fly seemed to pause for a split second in the current. That's when the mouth of the fish opened and it sucked in the fly. There was no splash. The only disturbance was a slight bulge in the surface as the fly vanished. The fish, of course, thought it had just eaten a nice, fat, juicy insect. When Jeff struck, all the fish did was shake its head. It was when Jeff applied pressure that the trout became angry, very angry. Never in its long life had anything made it so angry. This fish wanted no part of whatever it was that was doing this to him. First, the trout began to thrash on the surface. Then, unlike many big fish it jumped. Not once, but three times. Each time there was a thunderous crash as it hit the water. Jeff knew he really had his hands full and was doing everything he could to keep from losing the fish. Next, the fish decided to swim to the Atlantic Ocean, and seemed in a very big hurry to get there. There was nothing Jeff could do to stop it. When the trout had taken all of the line off the reel the leader snapped and the fish jumped one more time as if to say, "sorry, fellow, but I'm tired of playing this game."

"Too bad, Jeff," Robert called out, "that was a big fish and I am sorry you lost it. But, there will be others."

"Thanks for your kind words," Jeff answered forcing a smile, "but you can't win 'em all. Besides, it was a thrill just to have hooked a fish like that."

"Let's go on upstream to the next good run. It begins at the tail of the next pool."

As they walked the short distance upstream, Jeff could not help thinking what a beautiful morning it was.

"Here we are, Jeff. How does this pool look to you?"

"Fantastic," was the only reply he could come up with.

"Oh, look," Robert said in a hushed voice. "Right there at the tail of the current where it sweeps around that log, I think I just saw a trout rise."

Just as Robert was speaking, there was another rise.

"Boy, I saw that rise," came Jeff's excited reply, "and it looks like there are a few mayflies beginning to hatch out. See, just out from the log, there are a couple fluttering on the surface."

There was another rise as one of the mayflies disappeared.

"It looks like this might be the beginning of a good hatch," Robert said.

"It's your turn to fish, Robert. Do you know what pattern to use?"

"Yes, I think so. From here, it looks like one of the more common mayflies that hatch on the river at this time of year. I'll have to change flies," answered Robert as he took a size fourteen, light gray-colored fly from his fly box, and showed it to Jeff as he tied it onto his leader.

This time, Jeff stood on the bank watching, as Robert waded out into casting position.

The slanting rays of the morning sun filtered through the line of trees on the far side of the river, dappling the water with various shades of gold. Again, Jeff could not help thinking what a beautiful morning it was. He became aware of the riverside smells, the dew on the grass, the smell of the willows, wild mint, and the water itself. There were other smells, too. Smells he was not familiar with, but just as pleasant. Jeff loved the smells associated with a trout stream. Smells were every bit as much a part of the total fishing experience as the fishing itself.

Robert had begun to false cast.

"Wow," he yelled, "the insects are really starting to hatch and look at all of the trout rising." His fly landed softly and did not float more than a few inches before a nice brown trout had it. Unlike rainbow's, brown trout don't often jump. They seem to prefer to do most of their fighting beneath the surface. This one, though, was different. It jumped as high and often as any rainbow, before it decided to change its tactics and go deep. It became a kind of tug of war with the trout probably having the advantage, until the pressure of the rod finally began to wear the trout down. Jeff could see the tension on Robert's face ease. The fish was on the surface now, lying on its side. It only struggled slightly when Robert bent down to remove the fly from its jaw. He quickly lifted the fish for Jeff to see and then began to work the fish back and forth with its head facing into the current to revive the fish. It wasn't long before Robert felt the strength begin to flow through its body. It

Jack L. Parker

was not until he felt the fish was fully recovered, before Robert released his grasp. The fish, seemingly unafraid, swam slowly away.

"That was a really nice fish, Robert. How big do you think it was?"

"About twenty inches, and it was as fat and solid as any trout I have ever landed," Robert answered wearing a huge grin.

"It looks like there are at least a dozen or more fish still rising in that stretch. Try for another one, Robert."

"But Jeff, it's your turn."

"No," Jeff, answered, "I can see a lot of fish rising up near the head of the pool. Why don't you stay where you are and I'll go up and see if I can fool a couple of those guys. I found some flies in my box, like the one you are using, and I'll tie one on real quick and get to work."

It wasn't long before Jeff was knee deep in the river and busy casting to a rising fish. He had not made many casts before his rod had a good bend in it from the weight of a fighting trout.

After a nice tussle, he released a brown trout that would have to do a lot of growing to reach the size of Robert's twenty-incher. Glancing downstream, Jeff could see his new friend was fighting another fish and like before seemed to have his hands full.

Robert saw Jeff was looking at him and gave him a quick wave, which Jeff returned. Fishing up through the head of the pool, Jeff rose and hooked several fish. Some he was able to land, while others won their freedom before he could release them himself. Three of those fish broke his leader taking the fly with them. Looking into his fly box, he found he only had two of the gray flies left, and he soon lost one of those when a heavy fish took the fly and snapped the leader. Jeff never even saw the fish, but knew by its weight it had to have been a good one.

"I think that was another very big fish," Robert said surprising Jeff, who was just standing in the river with a real dumbfounded look on his face, after the trout broke off the fly.

"I didn't even see you come up. I don't know how big it was, but it did feel like it was a good fish. I've hooked some pretty nice fish in this stretch, both rainbows and browns. The biggest fish I released was probably about eighteen inches. I think the fish that just broke off was quite a bit bigger than that. I've got to tell you, Robert, this is one heck of a river. How did you do? It seemed like every time I looked down your way you were either fighting or releasing a fish."

"Like you, I did pretty well. I didn't land or even hook a fish as big as my first one. I lost the last pattern that matched the hatch and tried a couple of others, but the fish would not even look at them. It's like I told you, when these fish are taking a certain insect, it is really hard to get them to take anything else. Anyway, I thought I would come on up to see how you were doing. By the way, are you getting hungry? It's lunch time."

"You bet. Fishing always gives me an appetite. Besides, it looks as though the hatch is just about over."

"I'll tell you what. Let's go on back to where the

horses are and have lunch. After lunch we can fish for another hour or so and then head back. I have to meet with Tomas this afternoon about setting up the tents and other things for the auction guests."

"I'm with you. Besides, I've lost all but one of those gray flies myself and I don't want to lose it if I can help it. When we get the chance I will tie up some more and start teaching you to tie at the same time. And because it looks like the hatch is about over, the fish may take something else after we eat."

Back at the horses, Robert quickly built a small fire. He took a small flame-blackened kettle from a saddle-bag, filled it with water from the river and placed it over the flames to boil. In the meantime, Jeff had laid out their lunch on a flat rock, which consisted of several kinds of fresh baked bread, salami, and several kinds of cheese. "A meal fit for a king," was Jeff's comment as they began eating.

"Now, it's time for maté," Robert announced when they were both full. He took two gourds, silver straws and two small bags from the saddlebags. After removing the tops from the gourds, he took some of the dark green maté leaves from one of the bags and carefully tamped them into one of the gourds with his thumb, and told Robert to do the same with the other gourd. From the other bag, he poured some sugar into the gourds. Next, he took the kettle off the fire and poured boiling water into each gourd. The rich aroma of the steeping maté filled the air.

After replacing the tops to the gourds, Robert said, "A toast to new friends."

"And, to trout fishing and Patagonia," Jeff added sincerely.

They sat on the rock sipping their maté for several minutes looking at the river, each deep in his thoughts. It was a pleasant time for them both and Jeff actually enjoyed his maté.

It was Robert who spoke first. "If we want to fish some more we had better get to it. I think I will fish right here, Jeff. What about you?"

"I might just go right downstream and fish that riffle. How long do we have before we should head back to the estancia?"

"We should be back within two hours," Robert said checking his watch, "so by the time we take down our gear and the ride back, I would say that leaves us an hour to fish."

"I will meet you right back here in exactly one hour," Jeff replied as he checked his watch with Robert's.

As he was about to enter the water at the head of the riffle, Jeff glanced upstream towards the mountains. The storm clouds he had seen earlier were closer, but still a long way off.

Like Robert said, the storm probably won't reach us until sometime tonight, Jeff thought, as he changed from the dry fly he had been using to a good sized buggy-looking nymph he found in his box of wet flies. He also changed to a much heavier leader. As he told Robert, his favorite method of fishing was with a dry fly, but his second most favorite way, was to swing a nymph downstream in the current, and this stretch of water looked perfect for just that method. The technique seemed to work best in riffle water just like this.

It was not a very long piece of water and even in the deepest parts it did not look to be much over knee deep. Several good-sized boulders were scattered throughout the riffle offering the trout good shelter from the current. Jeff knew from past experience, trout living under these conditions were usually not very selective. They were opportunists. Because of the current, they did not have time to closely inspect their food. They had to grab it while the grabbing was good. And when they grabbed it, there was usually no messing around. They really grabbed it hard. The strike of even a ten-inch trout was a good jolt and look out when a really nice fish struck. It could be very exciting.

Facing downstream, Jeff began casting down and slightly across stream. When the fly sank he would let it swing until it was straight below him. Then he would let it just kind of hang in the current for several seconds. If a fish had not taken the fly by then, he would begin to bring the fly upstream towards him in a series of jerks. It was only a couple of casts before his rod was almost wrenched from his hand by the violent strike of a trout. He could tell right away it was a very big and powerful fish. In this kind of water, even a much smaller fish, had a good chance of freeing itself. Not only was Jeff fighting the fish, but the swift current as well. Sometimes, though, the pendulum can swing in favor of the angler, and this seemed like it might be the time it would swing in Jeff's favor. He did everything right, while playing the fish. He was able to splash to shore without falling in and follow the trout downstream when the fish decided it was high time, like the other big fish, it headed for the Atlantic Ocean. On one of the trout's rare jumps, its heavy body landed on the leader. The leader should have parted, but it didn't. It was near the end of Jeff's hour of fishing time, when the fish finally rolled on its side and he was able to lead the trout into quiet water. Looking at the fish his knees began to shake. He had a hard time removing the fly from the fish's jaw, because his hands were shaking even harder than his knees. Never, in all his years of fly fishing had he seen a trout as big as this one. Not even in Tibet. He decided to measure the fish while it lay still in the quiet water. Since he didn't have a ruler of any kind, he used the leader. He placed the end of the fly line where it connected to the leader at the fork of the tail and stretched the leader along the side of the fish to the tip of the jaw, where he quickly tied a knot. Later, back at the house the length of the fish would prove to be just a hair over twenty-five inches—one of the three largest fish ever recorded being caught on any of the estancia's waters. Robert, told him Tomas found one larger by nearly five inches in the river several years before, but that fish was found dead, on a sandbar. Tomas, assumed the monster probably died of old age and was washed up on the sandbar, during high water, caused by heavy rains.

Even though it had been a long, hard fight, it did not take long before Jeff's efforts to revive the fish paid off. The first sign was a sudden shudder, which traveled the length of its body. Its tail and fins began to quiver. It began to struggle, trying to free itself for Jeff's firm, but tender hold. When Jeff released his hold, the fish began to swim slowly, purposefully. It seemed to know exactly where it was going. Jeff only blinked once and the fish was gone. He stood glued to the spot, staring into the river where he last saw the fish. He began to doubt there ever was such a fish. Maybe he had only imagined it all. Maybe he was under some kind of Patagonian spell. He shook his head several times, and even went as far as to pinch himself to see if he was awake or not. "I'm awake," he said out loud, when he felt the sharp pain from the pinch. That's when he remembered the leader. Yes, the knot was there, he had not been dreaming. He was not under some kind of spell. He had actually just caught and released the biggest trout he had ever seen. Probably the biggest trout he would ever catch in his life. Jeff opened his mouth as wide as he could and let out the loudest yell he had ever yelled. The only thing hearing the yell was the animal that had been watching him intently from near the top of the cliffs. The animal's reply was a screech of its own. Jeff, thinking it was probably his own echo, shrugged his shoulders and walked back upstream to meet Robert.

Chapter 12

Jeff waited until they were riding back before he told Robert about his big fish. Robert was very pleased and seemed even more excited than Jeff. When they were almost to the barn, Robert asked Jeff what he was going to do while he was meeting with Tomas. Jeff, told him it would be the perfect time to write some letters, one to his mother and one to Trudy.

Jeff had never been one to write letters. Even though there was a telephone at the estancia, he knew it was very difficult to get a call through, and very expensive to boot. No, he would write letters instead. After he got back to the house, like Robert suggested, he went to the library. He was sitting at the desk and had just finished the letter to his mother when Nina came in. She said Robert, was still busy and would not be there, but if he was hungry, would he like to join her for the afternoon snack?

"Yes, Nina, I am hungry and I would like very much to join you," he told her.

While the two of them sat eating, Jeff felt at ease, not the least bit self-conscious. That was the kind of place this was and the kind of people who lived there. The entire atmosphere of the whole place was warm and friendly. For some reason or other, Nina asked if Jeff had slept well the night before. He replied, although he had slept pretty good, something very strange did happen.

"What do you mean by strange?" she asked in a concerned voice.

Jeff went on to describe the incident about how he thought he saw someone standing on his balcony when he had to get up to close the balcony doors. "I guess they blew open, because of the wind. I told Robert about it this morning. He just kind of changed the subject, so I didn't think any more about out it...that is, not until you just asked how I slept. I guess I could have been dreaming or imagined it. I was half asleep when I shut the doors. What do you think, Nina?"

"I really do not know what to tell you, Jeff," Nina said seriously. "However, here in Patagonia, strange things have been known to happen. But," she added changing the subject, "you must finish eating. I have some work to do. Both your father and Robert's will be here for dinner tonight."

"How long will they be staying?" Jeff asked.

"It looks like they will leave sometime tomorrow morning and will return again on the next day. But, one never knows."

Jeff finished eating and went back to the library. He wrote his letter to Trudy and began to look through the many shelves of books. He wanted to find a book to read to help pass the time until dinner. It was, he found, a wonderful library. There were books on all kinds of subjects. Because he was a book-lover, the time passed quickly. Before he knew it, it was time for him to go up to his room and get ready for dinner. As he was about to go up the stairs, Robert came in with both their fathers.

"Hello, Dad, it's good to see you," Jeff said as he got a warm hug and hello in return. "Hello, Mr. MacLean, have things been going alright?" he asked shaking Mr. MacLean's hand.

"They certainly have Jeff," came the happy reply, "and I trust Robert has been taking good care of you. I know he is going to be rather busy for the next several days with Tomas getting things set up for the auction. I hope you won't get bored."

"Not a chance. Today, we went fly fishing for trout."

"Great," Jeff's father said smiling. "You see Mac, fly fishing is Jeff's favorite thing to do. His mother says he would rather fish than eat. But then eating does just barely take a backseat to fishing. If, while we are here and we get the time I would like to do some fishing, too. Anyway, Jeff did you guys catch anything?"

"Did we ever," Jeff answered. "The river we fished was absolutely fantastic. We caught some really nice trout and lost a lot of fish as well. Dad, you really do have to take some time, to go while we are here. And, believe me, they have plenty of equipment. Maybe, the four of us could go and we could make a full day of it?" It was at this point in the conversation that Robert told them about Jeff's landing and releasing his big fish. He asked Jeff if he had measured the length of leader yet. Jeff said he hadn't, but if Robert would get a ruler, they would do it after dinner.

When they were about finished eating, Robert said, "Oh Father, I'm afraid I have some rather bad news."

"What do you mean, Son? What is it?"

"Tomas told me this afternoon, one of the gaucho's had found another freshly killed animal. This time, it was a full-grown cow. It seems it was killed by the big puma."

"First it was sheep and now cattle. Next it will be a horse. This cat must be huge. Is the gaucho certain it was the big puma?"

"Yes, he could tell by the tracks. One of its toes on the left front paw was missing."

"Did he try and follow the tracks?"

"He did, but lost them right away. He told Tomas the prints just seemed to melt away."

"Just like all of the other times," Robert's father said shaking his head.

After dinner the four of them sat in the library talking. It was late, nearly midnight, when they all went to bed. Again, Jeff was asleep almost before his head hit the pillow. It wasn't long after he was asleep that the storm struck. It was sometime during the darkest part of the night, with the storm at its peak, when Jeff was startled into consciousness as a tremendous blast of thunder shattered the air. Flashing lightning lit up his room.

"This is certainly no night to be out," he muttered, as he pulled the covers up closer under his chin. He sank into a fitful sleep. Tossing and turning, he began to dream. He dreamt someone, again, was watching him. Whoever it was, was dressed as a gaucho and stood motionless at the foot of his bed, staring at him.

Jeff sat bolt upright when there was a knock on his door. Bright sunlight streamed through the windows into the room.

"Get up my friend," Robert said when he came through the door, "it's a beautiful day. I've just been out to talk with Tomas. It seems he is going to be busy until this afternoon. So, I thought after a quick breakfast, we would take a ride."

"That's fine with me," Jeff answered rubbing his eyes and yawning. "Where to? Any place special?"

"For one, I want to take you farther up the river. Then we may just kind of roam around so you can see some more of the country. We won't be doing any fishing, but I will have Nina make us a nice lunch to take with us."

When Jeff, droopy-eyed, stumbled to get his clothes out of the closet, he almost stepped on a large, bright colored piece of cloth lying on the floor near the foot of his bed. It was soaking wet. He picked it up carefully by a corner, looked at it and asked Robert if he knew what it was, because he sure didn't.

"That's a panuelo, or neckerchief, like the gaucho's wear," replied Robert. "But what is it doing there?"

"I don't have the slightest idea. I've never seen it before. And look. Look here all across the floor. Those look like wet footprints and they lead out onto the balcony," Jeff said anxiously as he hurried to open the balcony doors. The balcony was empty, and there was no way anyone could get to it from outside—it was just too high above the ground.

While he was getting dressed, Jeff told Robert about his dream. Now, though, he said he was convinced it was not a dream. Robert couldn't offer any kind of explanation. He could not explain how the neckerchief got there.

When they got downstairs, Nina told them their fathers' had left early. They were anxious to see if the storm had caused any damage to the work in progress.

As they left the house for the barn, Jeff asked Robert to go with him and check out the flower bed located under his bedroom balcony, just in case. Even though the soil was muddy from the rain, they could not see any footprints or any other sign of the area having been disturbed in any way. He might have been able to shrug it off if it hadn't been for finding the neckerchief.

At the barn they both immediately noticed the look of concern on Tomas' face.

"Is something wrong, Tomas?" Robert asked him.

"A second cow has been killed."

"Another cow? When?" Robert asked with deep concern.

"Early this morning, not far from the river. It seems this thing kills for the pleasure of killing. I think this is a very dangerous animal," Tomas told them in a hushed tone.

• • •

Robert led the way. It was a perfectly clear morning. The distant snow-topped mountains seemed no more than an easy jog away. Looking up into the sky, Jeff saw a condor lazily wheeling round and round, going higher and higher, until it was no more than a tiny black speck. They were following a narrow trail through rolling country covered with lush, green grass. The smoothness of the landscape was broken up here and there by patches of large trees and head-high brush. It was, as they were passing one of the clumps of brush, when Jeff heard the sound of a bird singing.

"What kind of bird is that?" he asked, "It sure can sing."

"That is a calandria. Let's stop for a minute and listen to it. Maybe we will even get a look at it."

It wasn't long before Robert pointed to a little gray bird sitting on the end of a thin branch, not far away. It had black on its wings, sported a rather long tail, and was singing its heart out.

"For such a little guy, he can sure belt out a tune," Jeff whispered, so he wouldn't scare the bird off.

"Yes, he is the best singer in Patagonia. He can even mimic other birds. I have never heard it, but I have been told it can whistle like a human."

In a few minutes the calandria, cocked its head and it looked at the guys, as if to say, "Okay, fellows, the show is over," then gave a flick of its tail and flew off.

They rode on. Eventually, Robert turned off the trail and headed up the side of a heavily forested hill. At the top of the hill, they broke out of the trees and stopped. Below them, ran the river. From their high vantage point, they had an exceptional view. Jeff, speaking in low tones, told his friend what they were looking at had to be one of the most beautiful sights on earth. A trout fisherman's *dream river*, he called it. A series of

long, deep pools, were separated by sections of splash-
ing, rock-studded riffles, and sweeping glides. The
water varied in color from a deep green in the pools to
almost no color at all in the shallower parts. He told
Robert he felt this stretch of river even looked better
than the one they had fished the day before.

"Look," Jeff said, as he made a sweeping motion
with his arm, "look at the different colors of the river.
The colors remind me of the colors of different kinds
of precious stones."

"You know," answered Robert, "I've never looked at
it that way, but you're right."

"The color of precious stones, for a precious river,"
Jeff said.

On the other side of the river, the ever-present line
of cliffs seemed even higher and more rugged than
when they were farther downstream. There were wide
bands of green and pink rock running parallel to each
other. Looking up, Jeff could see a cluster of castle-like
pink stones perched precariously on the cliff's edge.
And here, upriver, just like Robert had told him, the
face of the cliff was even more pitted with the openings
of caves in all shapes and sizes. Jeff, saw how intently
Robert was studying the face of the cliff and knew he
was looking for some kind of sign or clue that might
show one of the caves was the den of the big puma.
That, too, is when Jeff noticed Robert had a holstered
pistol on his belt.

"Gosh, Robert, I didn't notice until now you were
carrying a gun," Jeff said.

"Tomas, gave it to me before we left. He feels very

strongly about this cat being dangerous. He said he would feel better if I took it along with us."

Since they weren't going to be fishing, Robert suggested they ride around so he could show Jeff some more of the country. They would have lunch somewhere and then head back to the estancia. As they were riding out of a wooded area, onto a small meadow, Robert stopped and looked off to his left towards the top of a bare ridge.

"Jeff," he whispered, pointing, "look at that."

"Oh, wow!" Jeff whispered back, "Would you look at the size of their antlers?"

"Those are red deer and they are both really big stags."

"What kind of deer did you say they are?"

"Red deer. They were imported to Patagonia many years ago from Europe, and have done really well here."

"They are magnificent," Jeff said, "just plain magnificent."

The stags stood on the ridge top for several minutes, with the deep blue Patagonian sky as a background. There may have been a shift in the wind and they got their scent, because suddenly, both stags gave a loud snort and quickly disappeared over the other side of the cliff.

As they continued on, and were about to enter the trees and brush on the far side of the meadow, they heard a loud noise, and just barely caught a glimpse of some kind of animal as it crashed through the underbrush.

"What was that?" Jeff rather excitedly asked Robert.

"That," laughed Robert, "was a wild boar. Another immigrant from Europe."

"Man, he sure did take off."

"If we hurry," Robert said, "maybe we can see it when it breaks out of the brush on the far side." He added, saying it would be a lot quicker for them to go around instead of through the thicket. He spurred his horse into a run and shouted over his shoulder for Jeff to follow.

"Let's do it!" Jeff yelled. All it took was a little nudge of his boot-heels and his horse took off like the wind, right behind Roberts. They got around to the other side and pulled up just in time to see the boar break out into the open at a dead run. The boar swerved off to the left, over a slight rise, and went crashing into another thicket, and was gone.

"Did you see that? I had no idea a wild pig could run so fast," exclaimed Jeff. "And did you see those tusks? They were mean looking. I certainly wouldn't want that thing mad at me."

"Yes," Robert answered, "they can run very fast and those tusks can really do a lot of damage. That was a big male. They have been known to charge when cornered, but a female with babies can be downright dangerous."

It seemed to Jeff it must be getting pretty close to time for lunch and so he asked Robert when they were going to eat.

"It won't be long now," he answered. "We're almost to the place I have chosen. I think you'll like it."

They entered another stand of trees and followed what looked to Jeff like some kind of animal trail.

When they reached the other side, they found themselves on the edge of a large, grassy plain. The plains gentle downward slope ended at the edge of a lake. As they walked their horses toward its nearest shore, the number of birds on the lake's surface amazed Jeff.

"Robert," Jeff stated, "look at all of the birds on that lake—there must be thousands. Do you know what kind they are?"

"Some of them I do, but not all of them. Do you see the ones out there where the lake is deeper, where the water looks dark blue? Those are what we call black-necked swans. In amongst the swans were various species of ducks."

"Would you look at all of those tall, pink birds wading in the shallow water on the other side of that low island? Are they by any chance flamingos?"

"Yes, that is exactly what they are and aren't they a beautiful sight."

"It's absolutely breathtaking. I've never seen so many water birds in my life," Jeff replied, "and all of those pink flamingos. It looks like someone has thrown a huge, pink blanket on the water. Do you think they will take off when we get closer?"

"No, I don't think so," answered Robert, "because you see they really never see many people here, so, I think they know they are safe. Do you see the clump of trees over there next to the lake? That's where we'll have our lunch."

As they rode towards the trees, Jeff's gaze focused on the far side of the lake where a vast forest of pine trees standing straight and tall seemed to march up the long sweeping incline, that ended at the base of the high mountains. An immense pile of whitish-clouds, hanging motionless as though being held by some invisible magnetic force, covered the tops of the mountains.

It was cool and pleasant in under the trees. A fire was going and the kettle was about to boil. They had finished eating and now it was time for maté. Each was sitting with their back to a tree, sipping tea from their gourd. This time, Robert had Jeff make the tea. He smiled and nodded his head in approval when he took his first sip and said to Jeff, "This is good maté, my friend."

"Why thank you, my friend, for the compliment," Jeff told Robert lightheartedly. "You know," he went on to say, "it looks to me like someone has used this spot before. There was already a ring of rocks for the fireplace and a nice pile of wood all precut. And, this big log we used for a table has been smoothed a bit on top."

"This is where my parents and my sister and I often come for a picnic, as you would say in your country. Tomas usually comes as well. He loves to cook over an open fire. Although we all enjoy birds, my mother is the real bird lover and expert in the family, and she is teaching my sister. As you have seen there are many kinds of waterfowl on the lake, as well as, several species of land birds in the area. She and my sister each bring binoculars and will spend hours studying birds."

"What do you and you're father and Tomas do?"

"Tomas paints. My father and I fish."

"Fish? Where in the lake?" Jeff asked rather puzzled.

"No, just over that little rise, a small stream enters the lake, but you can't see it from here."

"I assume, then this stream holds trout?" Jeff said teasingly.

"You bet it does," came Robert's firm reply. "Come on, let's walk over there. It only takes a minute."

They walked the short distance, through lush grass, to the top of the rise. Just below them, running through the meadow in a serpentine pattern, the little stream twisted its way down to the lake. You could follow its course by the scattered clumps of willows lining its banks.

"Gosh, you were right Robert, it isn't very wide is it? It sure is pretty, though. Look how it meanders its way through the meadow. This kind of stream can really be challenging to fish, because the trout tend to be really spooky."

"You've got that right, Jeff. The fish here are not easy to fool and you really have to be careful and not let them see you. Plus this little stream is very rich in insect life. See all of those beds of waterweeds in the stream? They are full of nymph life, and so of course, there are a lot of insect hatches. If you are fishing when there is a hatch of insects and the trout are rising to them, well, you had not only better have the right fly to match the hatch, but you must also present the fly perfectly. It can be very frustrating fishing. There will be trout rising all over the stream, taking insects off the surface, and I've had them ignore my fly and take a natural one within an inch of it, not only once, but several times. They seem to snub their noses at my fly. I'm sure if a fish could talk, they would laugh and say they were too smart for me. But, there are those times when everything seems to go right, and I have fooled them. When that has happened, I really feel good. There have even been those times when the trout in this stream seem to take any fly you offer them. That does not happen very often, but it has."

"I feel, anyway," Jeff, said, "that is one of the things that makes fly fishing such a great sport. You just never know what to expect."

As they stood looking at the stream, a few insects began to hatch out onto the surface of the water. It wasn't long before they saw the ring of a rise made by a fish as it gently sucked one of them in. Soon, there were a lot of insects hatching and more and more rings began to appear as more fish began to feed. It wasn't long before there were so many insects in the air, it looked like a miniature snowstorm was happening, and there were so many rings on the surface from feeding fish, it looked like raindrops striking the water.

"I guess now you can see what I mean, when I told you there were a lot of insects in this stream."

"And, it looks to me, by all of those rises, there are a lot of trout in this stream, too. I'm glad we didn't bring our fishing gear with us."

"Why is that? I thought you liked to fish."

"Of course I do. But, if we had brought our equipment, you would probably not have been able to pry me loose from the stream this afternoon, in time to get back to see Tomas."

"Oh, boy, speaking of Tomas," Robert said rather urgently. "We had both better pry ourselves away and get back to the estancia."

They were riding along the crest of a wooded ridge, when Jeff, looking down onto a flat clearing below, saw a solitary horseman stop at the edge of the trees and look around. Because of where they were located, the rider did not see them. Jeff pointed and they pulled up more out of curiosity than anything. It struck both of them that the figure looked vaguely familiar. When the person seemed satisfied, he spurred his horse into a trot, crossed the clearing and disappeared into the trees on the far side.

"Do you know who that was?" Jeff asked Robert with disbelief in his voice.

"Yes, I do. I wasn't sure until I was able to see the white spot on his horse's rump. It was the 'evil-eyed' gaucho."

"He sure was acting suspicious, the way he looked around before he crossed the clearing. I wonder what he's up to?"

"I don't know, my friend," answered Robert with pursed lips, "but you can bet he is up to no good."

Chapter 13

"Well," Jeff asked Robert after dinner, "how did things go with Tomas this afternoon?"

"Great!" Robert answered enthusiastically. "Things are going right on schedule. The tents will be put up next week and tomorrow we are going to play polo. Would you like to watch?"

"You bet I would. When are you going to play?"

"After lunch." Robert said, "We will practice in the morning."

"Good," Jeff replied. "Because I was going to go jogging in the morning. By the way, who is on your team, anyway?"

"Our regular team is made up of myself, my father and two of the gauchos, Carlos and Alex. Remember you met them both. They are the two who held the one-eyed gaucho from getting to Tomas. Actually, the one-eyed gaucho, was probably lucky, because even at his age and the condition he is in, Tomas is not a man to mess with."

"Will your father be here for the game?"

"Yes, both our father's are coming back around mid-morning."

"That's great. By the way, who are you going to play?"

"A team from another estancia," Robert said.

"Another estancia, huh. Have you played them before, and where the heck is this estancia, anyway?"

"Yes," Robert replied patiently, "we have played them before. In fact, we play them fairly often. Their estancia is located south of us."

"How far do they have to come, to get here?"

"Not far," Robert answered. "Well," he continued, "not far for Patagonia, anyway. If the road is clear, they can drive the distance in about two hours."

"Will they bring their own horses or will they be using yours."

"Actually, they will bring their own horses. These are the horses they will offer in the auction and they will leave them here with us. It would not make much sense to bring them back, when they can just leave them. They should arrive here sometime in the morning, and Tomas is going to do an asado."

"An asado?" Jeff questioned. "What's an asado?"

"It's meat roasted over an open fire. I think, because of the number of people, Tomas will probably roast a lamb and a calf. Believe me, Jeff, when I tell you, the taste is absolutely fantastic."

"When you put it that way, and even though we've just had dinner, I can hardly wait. By the way, Robert, how about me tying some flies and giving you a lesson, as well, before we go to bed? I would really like to tie up some of those flies we used on the river."

"A great idea," Robert answered enthusiastically.

In the game room, Jeff searched through the various drawers of fly tying materials until he found the things he needed to tie the pattern he wanted to tie. He laid the materials out neatly on the table and set up the vise.

"Robert, I think," Jeff said, as he sat down at the vise, "the materials I've laid out are what I need to tie that light gray-colored mayfly, so here goes. What I would like you to do," he added, "is just sit and watch me very closely and see how I go about it. I'll tie up a few for each of us and then I'll show you the basic steps. Now, don't expect to do well right off the bat, because it does take practice. I've been tying for a long time and the flies I tie usually leave a lot to be desired. But, every once in a while they catch a fish."

Robert sat at Jeff's side watching intently. As Jeff tied, he explained to Robert just what he was doing and why. He also told him the names of the different materials he was using. After tying several flies, he handed Robert half of them to put in his fly box.

"Now," he told Robert, "it's your turn. Even though you've been watching me and know the various steps it takes to tie a dry fly, I'm not going to start you out tying the same pattern I just tied. I will start you out tying a very simple fly that does not have wings like this one," Jeff explained, holding one of the flies he had just tied. "You see, to tie a fly with wings can be a bit tricky. So, the fly I am going to teach you to tie only has a tail, body and a hackle. The steps will be exactly the same the only difference will be the wings. The fly I am going to show you how to tie, like I said, does not have wings. And, of course the materials are different."

"Sounds good to me, the simpler the better."

"I think the best way is, I will tie the fly first, and then have you do one for yourself."

When Jeff was finished, Robert took his place. On his first couple of attempts, Robert seemed to be all thumbs. Slowly, he began to get the hang of it and the last fly he tied before they decided to call it quits, Jeff told him was very fishable and went on to say kiddingly, "The fly you have just tied is a very respectable and artistic endeavor, and one I am sure would fool a trout, though, perhaps not the most intelligent trout in the river. However, somewhere, yes, somewhere in the river there is a trout that will be fooled by that fly. But, all kidding aside, Robert, you did really well, one heck of a lot better than I ever did, when I first learned to tie."

Robert, felt a real sense of accomplishment. He knew he had a lot to learn and a lot of practice ahead of him before he could become a good tier. He told Jeff he had really enjoyed his lesson and appreciated Jeff's patience. He said he even welcomed Jeff's compliments.

Bright moonlight streamed through the balcony doors and windows of Jeff's bedroom. It was well after midnight when he woke. What woke him from such a sound sleep, he didn't know, but something did. It was a gradual awakening, not the kind where you are startled and lay confused trying to sort things out. This was by degrees, until he lay fully alert, to find himself staring up at the ceiling of his room. Slowly, purposefully, he lowered his gaze until it was centered on the foot of his bed.

The gaucho stood ramrod straight, his eyes locked with Jeff's. Jeff felt no fear. There was no urge to hide under the covers or to run out of the room. There were no chills running up and down his spine. Why he had none of these feelings was a bit of a puzzle. What he did know or feel was calmness, even curiosity. It was the look on the face of his unexpected visitor that struck Jeff most. At first, the strange figure wore a pleasant, friendly expression. This look changed shortly to a pained look or one of grave concern. Jeff was mystified with the change. He could not understand why. Then he began to feel the gaucho was trying to tell him something. Trying to warn him, but of what? Jeff was about to ask when the figure began to wave his finger back and forth and shake his head from side to side in warning. Again, Jeff was about to ask what the figure was trying to tell him, but it was to late. The gaucho turned and seemed to glide, rather than walk towards, and vanished through the closed doors to the balcony.

Jeff lay in a dazed state for a long time, but finally drifted back into a light sleep. His last thoughts were the words Nina had said to him about how in Patagonia, strange things have been known to happen. "Boy," he managed to mutter, "how right she is."

Chapter 14

When Jeff got up, he put on some shorts, a sweatshirt and his jogging shoes. As he was about to leave the room he happened to glance at the table where he had put the neckerchief. It was not there...it was gone! He knew he had seen it last night when he went to bed, but now it had disappeared.

Jeff turned on his heels and went straight downstairs to breakfast. He was determined to find out what was going on, and he was pretty sure Robert had been holding something back from him.

Robert had just sat down at the table, when Jeff strode in. He could tell by the look on Jeff's face something was wrong and said, "What is it Jeff? Is there something the matter?"

"Well, since you asked, yes there is something wrong, but I was going to tell you anyway," Jeff answered in a serious voice.

"Then tell me what it is."

Jeff, in minute detail, told Robert exactly what he

had seen in his room during the night. He was very firm about the fact he felt it was a ghost he had seen, the same one he had seen before. What he almost forgot to mention was that the neckerchief was gone. He was quick to point out it had definitely been on the table when he went to bed. He said he felt Robert knew more than he was letting on and Jeff felt he deserved a straight answer.

"Of course you are right. You do deserve an answer," Robert said, "so I will give it to you. On many occasions over the years, a strange ghost-like figure has been reported by many of our gauchos."

"What do you mean by that? Are you trying to tell me your house is haunted or something?"

"No, the ghost has never been seen in the house... that is not until you came."

"Well then, where has it been seen?" Jeff asked.

"Until now, he has always been seen out on the open range and always at night. He appears out of nowhere, riding a big Picazo."

"What the heck is a Picazo? Some kind of animal or something?"

"A Picazo, is a black horse with a white star on its forehead. The gauchos will be sitting around a campfire, and like I said, it is always at night when he just appears on his horse at the very edge of the light of the fire. He will get off his horse and join the gauchos. He never speaks, but always wears a friendly smile. At first the gauchos were afraid, but they soon realized he meant them no harm. He just seemed to want their company, to sit amongst them for awhile, to be with them."

"Man, that is really pretty spooky. Have you ever seen him yourself?"

"As a matter of fact, I have," answered Robert. "The first time, I was very young. My father and I were camping by the river. We were sitting around our campfire drinking maté. I remember it like it was only last night. It was a very still, warm, and dark night. The sky was cloudy so there was no light from the moon or stars. Only from the fire. It was just like the gauchos said. All of a sudden, there he was sitting on this big Picazo, right near the edge of the light of the fire. There was not even the slightest sound before they appeared."

"What did he do?" Jeff whispered tensely. "Just sit there on his horse?"

"No," Robert said, "he got off his horse and came and sat by the fire across from us. At first, I was really scared, but I soon realized there was nothing to be afraid of. My father even seemed to know him."

"And then what happened?"

"He sat there with a contented look on his face while we drank our maté."

"You didn't feel uncomfortable at all."

"No, not after I realized there was nothing to fear. After we finished our maté, he slowly got to his feet, looked at us, smiled a friendly smile, gave a little wave of his hand, which my father returned, and then my father whispered something I will never forget."

"What did he whisper?"

"He whispered, 'Goodbye old friend.'" Then the gaucho got on his horse and vanished."

"Did your father say or do anything else?" asked Jeff anxiously.

"Yes he did."

"Well, come on, out with it. What was it?" urged Jeff, who was now sitting on the very edge of his chair.

"My father told me very frankly, that what we had just seen truly was a ghost. He was also quick to tell me, if I should ever see him again, I should not be afraid. The ghost was very lonely. But he wanted us to know he was there to protect us if we should ever need his help. That was when I found out who the ghost actually was, because my father went on to tell me about the American gaucho and how he had saved his life two times. The first time, was when his horse strayed into the quicksand. The second time, he told me the gaucho not only saved his life, but the life of my grandfather and Tomas, when they were caught in the landslide. He said that was when the gaucho was killed and said he was riding the same big Picazo we had just seen him on."

"You said, the first time you saw him, you were very young. Have you actually seen him more than once?"

"Oh yes, but I really don't know how many times I've seen him. I have seen him when I have been out camping with the gauchos, and when I have been with my father like on the first time, and also, when I have been camping out by myself."

"Boy," Jeff said shaking his head slowly, "that is really some ghost story. But, do you know something; I did not feel the least bit afraid when I saw him either. Now, I guess I know why. Actually, I had the feeling he was trying to tell me something...maybe even warn me about something. Don't ask me what, because I certainly don't know."

"Wow," Robert exclaimed looking at his watch,

"I've got to get out to the barn, Tomas will be waiting for me. We have some things to go over before polo practice."

"I've got to get going as well," Jeff said.

"What are you're plans for this morning, Jeff?"

"I don't know if you noticed, but I didn't really eat much for breakfast."

"As a matter of fact I did," Robert answered smiling. "Are you sick or something?"

"No," Jeff said acting very serious, "I'm not sick or something. I'm going to go jogging, and I certainly did not want to have a full stomach. Even so, I think I'll take a brisk walk first and then jog. What time should I be back for the asado?"

"The asado will probably be ready around noon. We will hold a practice session before that. So, if you want to eat, be back at least by noon."

•   •   •

Jeff began walking at a pretty fast pace in the direction of the river. He walked until he felt it was all right to begin jogging. He followed the same route they had taken on the horses and it felt good to be out on his own. The air was cool, the perfect temperature for a good run. He had covered a lot of ground and was just coming to the top of a low hill, when he noticed several vultures circling lazily above a line of trees, not far away. Curiosity must have gotten the best of him, because he changed his direction so he could see if he could find out what the vultures were up to. At first, the going was kind of tough because the knee-high grass was pretty tangled. It wasn't long, though, before he reached a wide, swath-like trail that looked as though it had been made by something being dragged through the grass. He followed it through the trees to the edge of a gully that was heavily lined on both sides by dense bushes. Stopping near the edge of the bushes, he glanced at the ground and saw a line of small, dark spots he had not noticed before. What could they be, he wondered. He stooped down and touched a spot. It was still wet. At first glance, it looked like it might be blood. He rubbed it between his fingers and examined it more closely. Yes, he was sure. It was blood! This caused a feeling of anxiety to sweep over him and he quickly looked around. Jeff saw nothing unusual, only the buzzards circling over his head. He took a deep breath and began to follow the trail again. He did not know if the blood was human or animal, but told himself he had to know and would follow it until he found out. The trail led to a narrow opening in the bushes, at the edge of the gully. Very carefully, Jeff eased his body through the space. He lost his footing in the slippery grass and slid feet first down the steep incline and came to a stop just short of the bottom, which was muddy and full of some kind of high, thick, tangled reeds. Regaining his footing, he only had to continue following the trail a short distance before he found what he had been searching for.

Chapter 15

The calf was partially hidden in the tall grass. By its size, Jeff thought it was near fully grown, and by its looks, it had not been dead for very long. "Wow!" he exclaimed under his breath. "What are those tracks in the mud? Those are puma tracks, and one of the toes is missing off one of the paws. It's the same cat that has been doing all the killing and those tracks really look fresh. Uh, oh, what was that?" he said cocking his head. He thought he heard a rustling sound in the bushes on the far side of the dead calf. Looking closely, Jeff thought he saw a slight movement, but it could have been caused by the wind. There it was again, the rustling sound, but this time it was accompanied by a low, throaty, and thoroughly menacing growl. He stiffened, waiting. Jeff, who had been in some tight spots in the past, did not panic. He realized he had to keep a clear head. It was a matter of survival. If the big cat should charge, he knew he would not stand a chance. He had to stay calm. Slowly, carefully, Jeff began to back away, his gaze never leaving the spot where the sounds had come from.

"Don't run, don't run, take it easy," he kept whispering as he fought to keep control of himself. Jeff cautiously felt for each step, through the mud and tangled grass. He knew if he should fall, it would probably be all over. The big cat would almost certainly charge, and there was no way he could protect himself from the sharp claws and teeth of the killer. Inch by inch, step by step. The gap was slowly widening. It seemed like an eternity, but in reality, it was only a couple of minutes before Jeff felt he was far enough away to try and climb out of the gully. It was steep, but at least there were several exposed roots that would offer good footing and handholds. The last thing he wanted to do was to get part of the way up and slip back down again. As he fought his way up, he kept a sharp eye on the spot where the calf lay. When he was finally able to pull himself out onto flat ground, as tired as he was, Jeff did not hesitate. He began to run. He ran until he began to stumble, all the while he kept glancing back over his shoulder, just in case. At last he stopped to rest. He had no idea how far he had ran, but when he looked, he was surprised to find he didn't have far to go to reach the estancia.

Jeff made straight for the polo field. There were a lot of people and horses milling around, but it didn't take him long to spot Robert, who was just riding off the field with several others. He waved and called Robert's name to get his attention. Robert rode over, dismounted, and said he could tell by the look on Jeff's face something was definitely wrong and asked what it was.

As calmly as he could, Jeff told about his close call with the big puma. Robert, waited until Jeff was finished and then said in a low, serious tone, "Jeff, I do not know why the cat did not attack you, but you did the right thing by getting away from there without panicking. That's probably what saved you. Now, I've got to go to Tomas and tell him, so he can send some gauchos to check it out."

"Will they need me to show them the way?"

"No, they will not have any trouble finding the place. Besides," added Robert as he slapped Jeff on the back, "it won't be long before the food will be ready. I hope what you have just gone through hasn't taken away your appetite."

"I almost forgot about the asado, and to answer your question; no I have not lost my appetite. In fact, I'm so hungry I could almost eat your horse."

"Oh no you don't," Robert said acting as though he was protecting his horse with his body. As you know, Rabbit here, is my favorite polo pony. Besides," he added over his shoulder as he began to lead the pony away to go and find Tomas, "Rabbit would probably be too tough to eat anyway. And by the way, my father just went up to the house to take care of some things. He said to tell you your father wouldn't be here this afternoon because he had too much to do, but he said to tell you hello."

"Thanks. I guess I'll see you at lunch."

"Why don't you come on with me now so you can tell your story to Tomas yourself.

"He's cooking the asado on the other side of the building," Robert said pointing to a small building.

On the way, Robert asked one of the young boys, who was taking care of the horses, if he would take care of Rabbit.

As they rounded the corner of the building, the mouth-watering smell of roasting meat hit Jeff like a hard slap in the face. He had never smelled anything so good. Tomas, who was watching the meat very closely, greeted them with his normal warm smile. The look, however, soon grew grim as Jeff, related his story. When he had finished, Tomas excused himself, saying he would be back shortly. While Tomas was gone, Jeff asked Robert about the asado, and said it kind of reminded him of a barbecue back home, only this was on a much bigger scale.

"The asado," Robert said, "is more than just a barbecue. Here in Argentina, it is a tradition."

"What do you mean by that?" Jeff asked.

"First," replied Robert, "there is the fire and the meat, which as you see here is beef and lamb. Today, with the meat, Tomas is serving bread that is made here on the estancia and a green salad. Next, you have the clean, fresh open air and the cooking of the meat itself.

"Then, comes the actual enjoyment of the meal and visiting with the friends sharing it with you. After the meal is over, it is time for maté and more conversation. No, an asado must never be hurried. It is a time for pleasure. I guess you could say it is almost ceremonial."

"You certainly make it sound like it is. I was looking

at the beef and lamb, and how they are each mounted on a steel frame and seemed to be placed so they get just the right heat from the fire."

"Yes, to cook an asado takes much skill and patience. Tomas even has a secret recipe for the sauce he bastes the meat with while it cooks. You noticed the iron frame the meat is mounted on?"

"Yes."

"The frame is called an asador."

At that point, Tomas returned and told them he had sent two gauchos to check out the puma's latest kill. He felt they would not encounter the cat.

"It is too smart," he told them shaking his head. "But now it looks as though the meat is done," he added with a grin, "so why don't you two go tell our guests, it is time to have food."

Among those visiting from the neighboring estancia, there were a number of gauchos and whoever else was able to attend. So along with both polo teams, there was quite a little crowd. It was easy to pick out the polo players by their dress of high leather riding boots, with spurs, white polo pants and numbered polo shirts. The shirts of the players on the home team were light blue with black numbers, while the visiting team's shirts were white with black numbers.

Jeff asked why a player wore a certain number on his shirt. "As you already know," Robert answered, "there are four players on each team. The players wearing numbers one and two are the forwards on the team, number three, is the pivot of the team, and is usually the best player and the team captain. The number four is the one who plays the back position."

"What are the responsibilities of each player?"

"Okay, polo is a pretty complicated sport, but I will put it as simply as I can. The job of number one, when on defense, is to ride off the opposing back and try to prevent him from being able to keep hitting the ball, without trying to stop him. On the attack, number one tries to give the opposite back the slip and tries to get him to ride away from guarding his goal, so the number two can score. The number two is usually the strongest of the two forwards, and the driving force in an attack on the opponent's goal. He's also the main goal scorer. Now, the number three, or the pivot, is usually, like I said, the team's best player and the captain of the team. He will often initiate the attack and his main purpose is to get the ball up to the forwards, and to also try and intercept or cut off attacks on his goal. The back, who is the goal defender, really has to be a reliable player. He has got to be a good and accurate hitter, especially with backhanders. His job is to pass the ball to number two. I've got to tell you though; these positions are flexible. The best polo is played using teamwork, and being able to switch and play the different positions during the actual match when you have to. There is no room for a player who plays only for himself. The players have got to work together as a team."

"Thanks, Robert, for the quick lesson; now I think I'll be able to enjoy the game a lot more. By the way, I see you are wearing number one."

"Yes, I am, and my father is wearing number four, Alex is wearing number two and Carlos, our captain, wears number three."

"Are Alex and Carlos the best players on your team?"

"You bet," was Robert's firm reply to Jeff's question. "Carlos carries a ten-goal handicap and Alex a nine. My father, in his younger days carried a ten-goal handicap, but now he's a five."

"Do you mean to tell me Carlos and Alex are actually that good? Are they good enough to play professionally in Europe?"

"Oh, yes. Both of them have had offers to play in Europe and make a lot of money."

"Why haven't they done it?"

"They said they prefer to stay here. They don't need that kind of money. They are happy just as they are. The same goes for Tomas," added Robert, "but in his case, it is his art."

"What do you mean?"

"Tomas has had European art dealers wanting to show and sell his paintings. They have told him they could make him a famous artist and he could make a lot of money."

"What did Tomas do?"

"He told them he did not need or want a lot of money, and the last thing he wanted was to be famous. He did not want to change the way he lived. Tomas was even asked by the Buenos Aires art dealer, who handles most of his work, to come there for an exhibit of his paintings, but he refused to go."

"One more thing," Jeff asked hastily. "What about the handicap in today's game?"

"Actually, because each teams handicap equals out to be the same there will not be a handicap. And now,"

Robert added, as he handed Jeff a long knife like the ones the gauchos all wore, "it's time for you to learn how to eat an Argentine asado."

"I'm game. Let's get to it," Jeff replied with a laugh.

Robert demonstrated how to place a piece of meat on bread, put a good size part into the mouth and with the razor sharp knife slice off the bite. He said to Jeff, half seriously, when Jeff was about to take his first bite, to be very careful not to cut off the end of his nose. Jeff, however, soon got the hang of it and was eating just like the rest of them.

During the asado, Robert took Jeff around and introduced him. He was very pleased by their friendliness and the sincerity in their welcoming him to Argentina. There was a lot of laughing and joking among them and the main topic of conversation seemed to be polo. When everyone had eaten their fill, it was time for maté and more talk. After the proper length of time, Tomas announced it was time for the polo match to begin.

The small crowd walked to the bleachers while the players went to the edge of the field where their ponies were waiting. Before mounting, they put on the various kinds of safety equipment worn by polo players. After mounting, the teams rode out onto the middle of the field where each team lined up on opposite sides of the centerline so they were facing each other for the throw-in by one of the two umpires. The umpire, dressed in black and white striped shirt, bowled the ball under-handed down the space between the facing teams and the game began to the sounds of the thunder of horse hooves and the sharp clack of the ball being whacked by a player's mallet.

Jeff was on the edge of his seat. He had never seen a sport played so fast and furious. It seemed at times as though the players and horses were only a blur as they twisted, turned, made harrowing stops, only to gallop off at full speed again in a dizzy flurry of swinging mallets and stampeding horses hooves. It was a contest of speed and skill, a contest demanding the utmost courage, and spectacular horsemanship. It was almost as if horse and rider were one. The players seemed to be able to anticipate each others moves, as though they had a sixth sense. It was spectacular. It was exciting and the small crowd loved every minute of it. Before Jeff knew it, the first chukka was over and the players were changing ponies. Jeff caught Robert's eye and gave him a thumb's up sign and a big grin that Robert returned.

The score on the scoreboard read two for the home team and one for the visitors. Even as unfamiliar as he was with the game, the teams looked to be very evenly matched. At the ten-minute halftime break the score stood at eight goals each. Robert told Jeff both teams were playing excellent polo and felt the winning score would only be by a goal or two. It was at that point the two gauchos Tomas had sent to investigate the puma's latest kill rode in. They said although they tried, they could find no trace of the animal. As before, it just seemed to disappear.

And so the match continued. In the last chukka the score was tied at ten to ten. When the umpire blew his whistle signaling the last chukka was over, the score was still tied at ten to ten. Jeff asked the person sitting next to him what happens next. Was the match to end at a tie? He told him, because the score was tied, they would play another chukka. If that chukka also ended in a tie, they would keep on playing extra chukkas until one of the teams came out ahead.

The players were on fresh ponies and lined up facing each other for the throw-in. The play was just as fast and exciting, if not more so, than the rest of the match had been. Both teams seemed to be outdoing themselves, but it was nearly the end of the chukka and neither team had been able to score. The crowd seemed to think a second overtime chukka would have to be played, when all of a sudden the visiting team was able to initiate an attack. They came thundering down the field, their number four player was on the ball.

When Robert tried to ride him off, at the last second, the opponent made a backhand swing with his mallet, making a beautiful pass to his captain. Their captain, a ten-goaler, was on the ball in an instant. Riding hard it took only one stroke. There was a sharp crack when the mallet came in contact with the ball. It was a long shot, but the ball made it through the goal posts with only inches to spare. This was polo at its best. The whistle blew only seconds later. It had been as well played a match as anyone could have asked for. When the players of both teams rode off the field there was a lot of handshaking and backslapping among them. It was a real show of sportsmanship and comradeship.

"How did you like watching your first game of polo? Was it exciting enough for you?" Robert asked Jeff after he was finally able to free himself from the rest of the players.

Jeff tried purposely to hold back his enthusiasm a little, but couldn't and said, "It was fantastic! And, as far as being exciting, there aren't many sports that could keep me sitting on the edge of my seat the whole time like this one did."

"That's great, I'm really glad you liked it. Now, I have to try and find my father. He's probably talking to his close friends. They will be leaving shortly to go back to their estancia. Like I told you, they are leaving their horses with us because they will be in the auction. Their estancia raises some of the finest polo ponies in all of Argentina, and bring very high prices."

"I guess I'll go for another jog, so I guess I'll see you later," Jeff answered.

· · ·

He began jogging toward the river. His goal was to make it to the top of the heavily wooded hill and the trail the river skirted. He thought, from the top the view of the estancia and surrounding country would make his efforts worth it. The climb turned out to be a lot tougher than it had looked. Because, the hill was so heavily wooded he had to keep zigzagging back and forth through the trees. This took a lot of extra time and added a lot to the actual distance to the top. At last, he broke out of the last line of trees. He had made it and the view, as he had hoped, turned out to be well worth it.

For several minutes, Jeff stood in the shade of a tree resting against its trunk, taking in the view. Looking down on the late afternoon landscape was like looking at a large, panoramic, picture postcard. Off to his right, a series of forest clad ridges ended in a long sweep at the base of the heavily snow-clad peaks of the Andes. Even as he watched, a huge bank of dark, threatening, clouds suddenly popped up over the peaks as though some great giant on the other side had given them a big shove. Spread out below was the estancia. The roof of the main house was a deep red in the reflected sun of late afternoon.

It was easy to see the double line of white tents where they had been set up for the auction guests. The patchwork of various barns, outbuildings, corrals, and fenced pastures eventually gave way to open range where cattle grazed. Just a bit to his left, green meadows gently sloped and rolled towards the flat, brown tablelands that would eventually come to a sudden stop at the Atlantic Ocean. At first glance, what appeared to be large patches of snow, turned out to be several flocks of bleating sheep, slowly munching their way across the meadow.

Jeff was enjoying the peace and quiet. The only sounds were the birds and the breeze as it rustled the leaves in the trees. Periodically, a heavier gust of wind would swirl around, first pushing at him one way and then pulling in another. He was about to head back down the hill when he happened to notice a movement in a grassy clearing not far down the hill from where he was standing. His body tensed, especially after what happened to him that morning with the mountain lion. Whatever it was that moved, was located in the shadow of the trees at the very edge of the clearing.

"Uh oh," he whispered to himself, "there it is again. Something is down there." His eyes fixed to the spot were he was finally able to make out the figure of a horse and rider. The rider appeared to be doing something, but he couldn't tell what it was. Jeff moved so the trunk of the tree hid his body, his eyes never leaving the rider. Now he could see that whoever it was, was looking at the estancia through a pair of binoculars. But why? Who was this person anyway, and why would he be checking out the estancia? Was it someone just passing through the area? If so, why was he way up here on this hill? It was a good thing Jeff had hidden himself behind the trunk of the tree, because for some unknown reason the rider suddenly jerked his head around and looked up the hill right at the tree where Jeff stood. Jeff was sure he wasn't spotted, but the rider quickly turned his horse and started off down the hill in the opposite direction Jeff had taken. That's when he saw the large white spot on the horse's rump. There was no mistake, it could only be one person—the evil-eyed gaucho.

Chapter 16

That night at dinner, Jeff was so tired he even forgot to tell Robert and his father about seeing the evil-eyed gaucho. The dinner talk was about the polo match and Jeff's father said more than once he wished he had been able to see it. After dinner they all went into the library to continue their talk. It wasn't long before Jeff found his eyelids getting heavier and heavier. He fought to keep them open, but it was a losing battle. It was Robert's father who suggested they all get to bed early, saying he and Jeff's father had to leave after an early breakfast.

The storm hit just as they were climbing the stairs to go to bed. Jeff did not need the sound of heavy rain on the tiled roof to lull him into a heavy sleep. He did not move until early the next morning, when Robert had had to shake him awake. When they got downstairs, they were both glad to see their father's were still eating. It was when Jeff and Robert had just about finished that Tomas came into the dining room with a grave expression on his face.

"What is it, Tomas? What's wrong?" Mr. MacLean asked in a concerned voice.

"Last night," Tomas began barely able to control his voice, "during the storm, three polo ponies were stolen."

"Are you sure they were stolen?"

"Yes," Tomas replied firmly, "there is no way they could have got out by themselves.

"It is bad enough that they were stolen, but to make matters even worse, two of the ponies were not ours. They were among those left by your friends to be put up for auction."

"That does make matters worse," Mr. MacLean stated firmly. "Those horses have got to be found."

"I have already sent out three groups of gauchos to begin the search. There is little hope though of finding them, because all traces of a trail would have been washed away by last night's storm. I do not know who would do this kind of thing, but whoever it was knew exactly what they were doing."

"Maybe I can help," Jeff said and told them about having seen the evil-eyed gaucho yesterday on the hill and how he seemed to be checking out the estancia through binoculars. "I kind of thought he was up to no good, but there was nothing I could do about it and I didn't want him to see me. There's no telling what he might have done."

"Well, that seems to settle the matter of who stole the horses," Mr. MacLean said shaking his head, and added, "You certainly did the right thing by not letting him see you Jeff, because like you said, if he had, there's no telling what he might have done."

"But, why would he steal polo ponies from you?" Jeff's father asked.

"To take across the border into Chile where he will sell them for only a fraction of what they are really worth," Tomas answered. "But, he can't get over any of the passes. They are not yet open because of the snow. So, that means, he probably has some place to hide them until the snow melts enough so he can make his escape."

"Do you have any idea when that might be?" Jeff asked.

"That is hard to say," Tomas replied. "But from what I have heard, it could be within the next week or two."

"It won't be that long before the first guests will be arriving for the auction. Those ponies must be found before then. I know you will do everything you can, Tomas," MacLean said. "But now Mr. Thornton and I have to leave. Keep me informed and good luck."

Every day, Tomas sent out search parties. This went on for several days. They never found a trace of the horses or the evil-eyed gaucho. There was talk about what might have happened to them, but of course, no one knew for sure. During that time, in the morning, Jeff was kept busy helping Robert and Tomas as they continued their preparations for the auction. In the afternoon he often watched as the team practiced polo. Usually, Mr. MacLean showed up for these, but would leave as soon as practice was over. When time allowed, Jeff would take a short jog or brisk walk. Late one afternoon he had the strong urge to go fishing. It had been in the back of his mind for quite awhile. He wanted to go as far upriver into the canyon and fish up as far as he could. When he asked, Robert said he was too busy, but Jeff should go ahead and go. When Jeff told Robert where he planned to go, Robert advised him strongly against it. "It could be very dangerous," Robert warned. "I don't know of anyone who has gone into the canyon any farther than where we fished. It's a place, for whatever reason, people just do not go. The gauchos don't even venture very far into the canyon."

"Have they gone into the canyon looking for the stolen horses?" Jeff asked.

"Not really, at least not very far. They felt the going was too difficult for someone to take three horses any farther than they went. But then I think they are rather superstitious about the canyon. I don't know why, but they are."

"I promise," Jeff, said seriously, "I will not do anything foolish. I plan to leave before daylight tomorrow morning and will be back before dark."

"Well," replied Robert, "if you really want to go, do me one favor."

"Sure, what is it?"

"Take a pistol with you. It would make me feel a lot better."

Jeff agreed and Robert said he would have Nina make him an extra big lunch to take with him.

He was up and had his equipment ready, his horse saddled, and was on the trail well before the sun's first rays began to creep over the distant horizon. One thing Jeff almost forgot was the pistol. He had to run back upstairs to his room and get it off the table where he put it when Robert gave it to him the night before. He slipped it into one of his saddlebags.

It was a crisp, clear morning. Jeff's horse was extra frisky and seemed as happy to be on the trail as he was. What it really wanted to do was run and Jeff had to keep a tight rein just to keep the animal in a gallop. They made good time. Even though, it was just beginning to get light, Jeff had no trouble finding the place where Robert told him to cross the river. Once on the other side, he began to follow the faint trail upstream—the trail that would take him deep into the canyon. What he thought he would try and do was ride into the canyon for two hours. That would give him plenty of time to fish before having to head back to the estancia.

When Robert asked Jeff why he wanted to go so far into the canyon to fish when there was such good fishing lower down, Jeff told him it was because he might be the first person to have ever fished that part of the river, and that he loved adventure.

Because it was so sure-footed, Jeff let the horse pick his own way. The going was far from easy and there were a couple of really rough places where he had to get off and lead the horse. After more than an hour, much to his surprise, the floor of the canyon actually widened and the going became a lot easier. Just before the two-hour time limit he had set, Jeff came to what he felt was the perfect place. He crossed a small stream that came out of a narrow break in the canyon wall and stopped under a tree in a grassy area at the edge of where the little stream flowed into the river. Before dismounting he just sat there taking in the scenery. It had turned into one of those beautiful, luminous, and serene mornings, with surroundings to match—an often-rare combination. There seemed to be the smell of growing things everywhere. The damp odor of mosses, the almost overpowering smell of wild spearmint, and other smells he was not familiar with, but they were just as pleasant. Here, along with the sound of the river and the birds, there was the sound of silence, a silence so profound you could actually hear it. Butterflies fluttered, weaving and dancing in the sunlight. Jeff, felt the warmth of the early morning rays of the sun on his back and he thought to himself just how good it was to be alive. There was the added surge of excitement in knowing he might be fishing unexplored waters. Looking up, he saw two huge condors lazily circling back and forth; the only dark specks against the sky.

The blackberry bushes scattered along the banks of the river, hung heavy with the pale red of un-ripened fruit. The edges and grassy areas along the river were bright with the colors of wild flowers in full bloom, and the willow and poplar trees were in full leaf. The faint smell of pine from somewhere farther up the canyon came wafting down on the morning breeze. At this point, the river's cold, clear current was strongest at the very center. There was a gentle curve toward the deeper water along the far bank, and the scattered heads of large boulders broke through the surface at just the right places. The near shore was paved with cobble-sized stones and sloped gently towards the edge of the fast current. Jeff was so engrossed with everything he almost forgot why he was there. It was the commotion of a large trout, as it tried unsuccessfully to grab an insect skittering across the water that brought him back to reality. It was time to go fishing!

After putting his tackle together, and tying on a large dry fly, he decided to begin fishing right there and work his way upstream until it was time for lunch.

Standing knee deep, he studied the river.

"There," he said out loud with more than a little excitement in his voice, "in that slick water behind that flat boulder. I think I saw a fish rise."

At first the cold water only pushed gently against his hip boots, but became stronger the farther out he waded. He found he had to be very careful, because the water was so clear, he had trouble gauging its actual depth. Once in position, it only took one cast to prove he had been right. It had been a fish and it really nailed the fly. It was not as big as some of the other trout he had caught in the river, but like the others, it was a strong, hard fighter. After he released the fish, Jeff began working his way slowly upstream, casting to the likely looking spots, when there came the sound of falling rocks from above where he had tied his horse. It's nervous stomping and snorting caused Jeff to wade ashore. By the time he reached the animal's side, it had quieted down so he went back to his fishing. The fishing was kind of slow. The trout seemed to rise to his fly just often enough to keep him on his toes. The blazing sun now beat down into the canyon. The combination of bright sun, heat and clear water, seemed to put the fish off their feed. After getting out of the water to walk around a deep pool, Jeff stood in the shade of a tree to change flies. He seemed to sense, more than see, the big boil on the surface, as a big fish rose just out and slightly upstream from where he stood. He made a quick cast. The fly floated over the spot, the fish rose, but did not take the fly. Another cast and the same thing happened. The fish rose, but snubbed the fly. Past experience had taught Jeff that when this happened, the thing to do was change to a different fly. He picked a large all brown fly from his fly box and quickly tied it onto the leader and made a cast. The fly seemed to tiptoe on the surface as the current carried it downstream. This time the trout rose in such a deliberate manner that when Jeff struck, there was no doubting the fish was well hooked. It came out of the water in a slow-motion arch, the color of a shimmering rainbow. Jeff could even see the fly in the corner of the trout's mouth. The big fish thrashed and lunged all over the pool and then went to the bottom where it sulked for several minutes. Nothing Jeff tried would even budge the fish. Suddenly, it seemed to have had enough and came alive. Upstream it streaked, causing the line to zing through the water and the reel to screech. When it reached the fast water above, the strong current did not slow the fish down one bit. One second there was the pull on the rod of the heavy, powerful fish and the next—nothing. The line went slack. Slowly, half dazed, Jeff reeled in the limp line. Had the fish only been hooked lightly after all and the fly pulled out? Had the leader broke? These thoughts raced through his head. When he checked the end of the leader, it was flyless, but the leader had not broken. In his haste to tie on the fly, the knot was not secure and had pulled loose—it had come untied. Losing the fish was his own fault.

"Well, Jeff," he muttered sarcastically, "I hope you've learned a lesson here today."

Looking upstream with the flyless leader still in his hand, he thought he saw another fish rise. It was hard to tell because it was in the shadow of a large log that lay at the edge of the current.

"Ah, ha," he whispered. "There it is again. That was definitely the rise of a fish." He picked another one of the all brown flies from his fly box, and this time after carefully tying it onto his leader, made very sure the knot was tight.

He had to get closer to make a good cast. Inching forward, the water came to only a couple of inches from the tops of his boots. "Take it easy," he said looking at the tops of his boots. "Only a couple of steps and I should be able to reach that fish." The sun on his back seemed even hotter. He was wiping the sweat that kept running into his eyes off his forehead when it happened. He was just about to take a step, when his feet began to slide. There was nothing he could do. Slowly, standing straight up, with his rod held high over his head, Jeff just kind of glided forward until he was up to his neck in the frigid waters of the river. Gasping, from the shock of the icy cold, he just stood where he came to a stop for a couple of minutes. There was no danger of drowning and the water even began to feel good, especially after the initial shock wore off. And, for some reason, he wanted to see if the fish was still rising. It wasn't. When he was satisfied the fish was not rising anymore, he worked his way to shore and sloshed to where he tied his horse. After taking off and empting out his hip boots, he stripped off his clothes and hung them on the branches of a tree to dry.

"Well," he laughed, "I guess I timed falling in just right, because I'm hungry and it's time for lunch."

First off, he gathered some dry limbs and started a small fire, and filled his pot with water form the stream. While he sat on a rock in the shade of a tree eating, his thoughts turned to Trudy and how she would laugh and kid him when he told her about his latest falling-in-the-river episode. After eating, he took his gourd and pouch of tea from the saddle, put the pot on the fire to boil and made maté. After a second gourd, he put on his clothes, which by now were dry, and decided to take a short nap. It was pleasant in the shade and he was soon asleep—but not for long.

The sound caused Jeff, to sit bolt upright. It took a few seconds for him to gain his bearings and to realize his horse was in a near panic with fright. It took quite a while to quiet the animal. Jeff had shrugged it off earlier when the horse was frightened. This time he got a little nervous. After several minutes of watching and listening with nothing out of the ordinary happening, he felt it was probably due to some more falling rocks. He shook off the nervous feeling and decided instead of fishing the river again, he thought he would check out the little stream. It was probably because of his sense of curiosity and love of adventure that caused him to want to check out the stream. He had plenty of time before he had to head back and he wanted to see if it held any trout.

The stream came tumbling out through a narrow cleft cut in the side of the canyon. What Jeff planned on doing, was ride up the stream as far as he could, exploring and maybe even fish a little. At first it looked like the opening might be too narrow for the horse, but when he tried, he found it was wide enough, so he did not even have to get off and walk. Once through the opening, the walls widened out, but he still had to keep to the stream. Large boulders had rolled down the streambed in some great flood in ancient times and Jeff had to tread his way though them. It wasn't long before he came out of the small gorge and rode into a miniature meadow valley, surrounded on all sides by high rock walls. For the moment, the stream held Jeff's attention, especially, when from the vantage point of being on his horse, he was able to look over a boulder into the pool. The water was tinged with just a touch of green for color. On the bottom of the partly shaded pool, he saw several trout where they lay motionless. When an insect would float over, one of the fish would slowly rise and pluck it off the surface.

Fighting the urge to fish, he rode ashore and headed his horse upstream. He rode through a small bunch of trees and when he reached the other side, pulled the animal to a sudden stop and exclaimed, "Wow, what is that?" in a startled voice.

Chapter 17

The valley looked like it wasn't too much bigger than the polo field back at the estancia. Against the back wall of the canyon was a makeshift corral. In the corral stood three horses. "Could these be the stolen polo ponies?" he whispered hopefully. When he reached the corral, he knew by the description he had been given, these were the stolen horses. There was feed spread out on the floor of the corral and a spring that formed a stream, gushed out of the side of the cliff into a pool forming a natural drinking trough for the ponies. Making a part of one side of the corral, with the rock wall at its back, stood a shabby one-room shack. Except for Jeff and the horses, the valley was empty. An almost supernatural feeling about the place slowly crawled over Jeff's body as he dismounted and walked to the fence of the corral. Even the horses seemed nervous. Jeff did not know what caused the feeling, but what he did know was he did not like it. The feeling seemed to become stronger as he hurriedly walked to his horse.

He had just put his left foot into the stirrup and thrown his right leg over the saddle, when the silence of the place was broken by a loud, piercing scream. Instantly, his horse began to buck in terror. Jeff automatically reached for the saddle horn—the saddle horn that was not there. For an instant he was airborne and then landed with a thud in a heap. He lay for sometime, dazed, with the breath knocked out of him. Finally, he tried to get to his feet, but his right ankle would not support his weight. Another scream split the air. This time it sounded much closer. His horse bolted in wild-eye terror towards the entrance of the valley. The horses in the corral would have done the same, but the fence was too strong for them to break through.

"Now what am I going to do?" Jeff wondered out loud. "I've really got myself into a mess this time. I guess I'll just have to make the best of it."

He knew he would at least have to spend the night. The only shelter was the shack. "Oh well, any port in a storm, as the old saying goes," he muttered as he painfully began to hobble towards the door. There was another chilling scream when he reached the entrance. Trying to ease his feeling of tension, he thought the noise might be caused by some natural phenomenon like the wind blowing between the rocks, but deep down, he knew it wasn't.

It was dreary and dingy inside the shack and it took a minute before his eyes adjusted to the dim light. He went and sat on the floor with his back against the rock wall. After some time, he drifted off into a nervous sleep.

It was after dark when Jeff woke with a start. Outside, the wind howled, lightning flashed and thunder roared. The sound of the storm was not what woke him, but something he sensed, rather than heard. His body stiffened. Something was just outside the door. There was a bright light, but not from lightning. The light came from a powerful flashlight and its beam was aimed directly into Jeff's eyes.

"So, it is you," the voice seemed to hiss, rather than speak. "You are the North American who is staying at the MacLean's estancia."

Jeff knew who it was, even before he saw the face, and answered, "Yes, I am staying at the MacLean's and they should be here at any time," he added bluffing.

"I do not think so—especially not in this storm. I thought someone had found my little hideaway, when I saw the panicked horse. I would have caught it, but I was coming from upriver when it burst out of the entrance and ran like the wind down the trail. It is a shame, because, yes, they will come searching for you, but certainly not until tomorrow. So, now I will have to move the horses to another place."

Jeff saw the glint of steel from the knife blade, the evil-eyed gaucho held in his other hand, and in a voice as calm as he could manage, said, "What are you going to do with me? They know you are the one who stole the horses, and eventually they will find you."

"Ha!" the gaucho said as he spat on the floor. "They will never find me. Besides, the snow on the passes will soon be melted. When it is, I will go to Chile where I will sell the horses. I will not have any problem hiding from your friends until then. And, now as for you, I have not yet decided just what to do with you. I cannot let you go," he said shrugging his shoulders and laughing his wicked sounding laugh. "But, what I think I will do is tie you up. If and when they ever find you, you may only be a skeleton. However, if they should by chance find you while you are still alive...well...like I told you, I will be a long way from here by then."

The gaucho swiftly stepped close to Jeff and held the knife within an inch of his throat. Jeff thought the gaucho was actually going to use it on him and the man seemed truly disappointed when Jeff did not plead for his life. Just as swiftly, he stepped back and glared hatefully at Jeff with his one good eye. He took the rope he had coiled across his shoulder and easily sliced it in two with the razor sharp blade. The sneer never left his face.

Thoughts kept racing through Jeff's mind. The one thing he knew he did not want to do was to make the gaucho lose his temper. After seeing what he did when he lost it in the barn, there was no telling what he might do if he lost it here.

"Roll over onto your stomach," commanded the gaucho, "and put your hands behind your back."

Jeff knew with his injured ankle, there was little chance of his being able to escape. He was about to roll over, when the night was shattered by another scream. This time it sounded so close, it almost knocked the gaucho off his feet, and the man let out a hoarse, fearful cry and blubbered something about a Devil Cat. Next, came a sniffing sound from just outside, followed by a low, throaty growl. The gaucho dropped to his knees unable to move. Suddenly, the huge shadow of the cat filled the doorway of the shack, and it raised its immense head to the sky and let out a scream so loud and terrible, it echoed off the canyon walls in spite of the noise of the storm. The gaucho, now reduced to a whimpering, helpless mess, crawled to the far corner of the shack where he lay on his side with his knees drawn up to his face, begging for mercy. For a few precious seconds, the gaze of the cat was on the gaucho. Jeff had just enough time to reach out and get the gaucho's knife, where he had dropped it when he fell to his knees. His hands were shaking, but now Jeff felt at least he had some kind of chance. He wished now, more than ever, he had the pistol Robert had given him, but it along with his knife was in his saddlebags. The cat's attention switched to Jeff, as it dropped into a crouch. Jeff pressed his body closer to the wall and held the knife ready for what he knew was about to happen. His body was soaked in sweat. The huge cat's eyes stared into Jeff's, never wavering, and its muscles tensed as they always do just before the leap.

• • •

It was at this same time, Tomas hurried as fast he could up to the main house. Both Robert and Jeff's fathers had returned that afternoon and were sitting in the library talking with Robert. They were all worried about Jeff's having not yet returned from fishing. Tomas told them in grave tones, how Jeff's rider-less horse had just ran frothing at the mouth into the stable. They all quickly agreed that to start a search at this hour, in such a storm, would be foolish. They would start at first light and could only hope Jeff was not seriously injured.

It might have been the extra bright flash of lightning, but the cat hesitated for just a second before leaping. And then it happened. Out of nowhere, the image Jeff had seen in his room appeared. The ghost of the gaucho stood between Jeff and the crouched cat. The creature shrank back, snarling and bellowed a scream, but this time it was a scream of terror. It spun around and fled through the door, leaving a deep trail where its claws had dug into the earth in its flight, never to be seen or heard from again.

It took several seconds for Jeff to gain his senses. He was still shaking, but the feeling of impending doom was gone. It was then, that the evil-eyed gaucho managed to slither out, and make for his horse, as fast as the scared, cowardly creature that he was, could. He had some trouble, because he had tied his horse so well, but finally, he tore the reins loose, jumped on and spurred the poor animal into a headlong run to get himself away from the place as fast as he could. The evil-eyed gaucho, like the puma, was never seen or heard of again.

The ghostly figure looked straight at Jeff, smiled, and said, "Set the bush at the entrance to this valley on fire when it is fully light. They will see the smoke and come for you."

"How can I ever thank you?" Jeff asked gratefully.

"I don't want your thanks," answered the ghost warmly. "I am from your country," he continued. "I came to Patagonia many years ago, long before you were ever born. What happened to cause me to stay here does not matter, but I died before I could ever return home to see my family again."

"Is there anything I can do for you?" Jeff asked hopefully.

"One thing, give your father this ring. He will know what it is and will give it to your mother," he said handing Jeff a gold chain with a small child's ring on it.

"But, what will I tell him about how I got it? Will he understand?"

They looked warmly at each other in silence. Somehow, Jeff had a strange feeling about the ghost, but he couldn't put his finger on it. What he did know was that he had a good feeling. It was as though they were enjoying each other's company, and nothing had to be said between them. Finally, the figure smiled another warm smile at Jeff, gave him a slight wave of his hand, and slowly melted away. Jeff tried to call him back, but it did no good. He was gone. There was another bright flash of lighting; followed by a clap of thunder so loud Jeff covered his ears. When the thunder stopped, so did the rain. The storm was over.

It was pleasant sitting in the light of the morning sun. Jeff's ankle was much better and he was able to walk out to the main river without much trouble at all. The bush was burning and a column of dark smoke spiraled its way into the cloudless blue Patagonian sky. Jeff knew he was very lucky to be alive. He began to examine the gold baby's signet ring, which was made in an unusual hexagon design. The ring looked familiar. On the flat surface, were the initials H.D.R.

"That's it!" he said excitedly slapping the side of his leg, as he began to remember, "This ring, it's the same kind of ring mother wears around her neck, and the initials on both rings are the same. H.D.R., those were her initials before she married dad and stand for Helen Dobbs Reeves." The name "Dobbs," Jeff knew was a family name on his mother's side. It had been her father's middle name. Because she was an only child and did not have a brother, the name was given to her. It was also Jeff's middle name. Was this some kind of weird coincidence or something, he wondered? He didn't know. He did know, his grandfather had supposedly died in some foreign country, but the family never found out for sure what really happened to him. He had been a geologist and traveled a lot to foreign countries. Jeff also remembered, once when he was young, going through an old trunk when they were visiting his grandmother. In the trunk, he found a bundle of letters from his grandfather. They were all from Argentina. When he asked his grandmother where Argentina was, he remembered when she told him, she had tears in her eyes. After that he always thought someday he would like to visit Argentina, and now, here he was.

It was shortly after mid-morning when Jeff heard the sound of horse hooves on the trail, just before his rescuers rounded a bend. Tomas was in the lead, followed by Robert and both their fathers. It was a happy reunion. They all started throwing questions at Jeff at the same time.

"Okay, okay," he said raising his hands for everyone to be quiet. "I'm going to tell you exactly how I came to be in this fix, but what I am going to say may sound pretty darned far-fetched, but believe me every word of it is true."

Jeff began telling his strange tale from when he woke up from his nap after lunch. The only time he was interrupted was when he told about finding the three stolen polo ponies. Other than that, his small audience was totally speechless.

When he had finished, he told them again how he thought they might not believe him, but it was all true.

"No, no, Jeff," Tomas said sincerely. "Myself and Robert and his father believe you. I know you know about the ghost of the North American gaucho, because Robert had to tell you after you saw him in your room. But, your father does not know, so I will tell him." Tomas went on to tell Jeff's father the same story Robert had told him, but added how the gaucho had visited Jeff that other time in his bedroom. When he was finished, Jeff's father just sat there shaking his head in wonder.

"Well, Son," Jeff's father began, "after the story Tomas has just told me, there is no reason why I should not believe you, but you know, I would have believed you anyway."

"Boy, am I ever glad. Because for a while there I thought I might have been dreaming or something. But when I saw the ring in my hand, and the huge marks the cat left in the dirt floor of the shack when it took off out of there, I knew it was true. Now," Jeff said, looking at his father, "I don't really understand about the ring. Like I said, it has Mother's initials before she married you, engraved on it. Here, Dad, you have a look at it."

"Jeff," replied his father, in a low, serious voice, "I don't have to see the ring. Does it have a date engrave on the inside?"

"Yes," answered Jeff as he read off the date.

"You see, Son, that is the date your mother was born."

"So, then this ring belongs to her?"

"No, as you know she wears her baby ring, which is the twin to the one you are holding, around her neck."

"I guess what you are saying then, is there are two identical rings. This one and the one she wears around her neck."

"Right."

"Well," Jeff began slowly, "if Mother has hers, who had this one?"

"Her father, who is, of course, your grandfather."

"Whoa," Jeff said hoarsely, his knees becoming week. "Do you mean to tell me the ghost who saved my life and gave me this ring, is the ghost of my lost grandfather?"

"I would be willing to bet my life on it," came Jeff's father's solemn answer.

"Gosh," was the only word Jeff was able to say.

"This finally cleared up a lot of things about the gaucho, for us as well," Mr. MacLean stated with a sigh.

"I can see how it does," replied Jeff's father to his old friend. "From what you've told me, it sounds like this gaucho was quite a man."

"Indeed he was," answered Robert's father, "indeed he was."

"Why," Jeff asked of his father, "did my grandfather come to Argentina in the first place?"

"Your grandfather was a well known geologist. He often went to other countries, usually at the request of the country's government, to search for various kinds of mineral deposits. That's why he came to Argentina, he was hired by the government."

"But why did he stay here and not come home?"

"That's a hard question to answer, Jeff, because no one knows. What might be the reason though, was he found some kind of valuable mineral deposit and met with some kind of accident or even foul play. It's not uncommon for a hit on the head to cause a person to lose his memory. Sometimes it is only temporary loss of memory, but sometimes it last for a long time and could even be a permanent condition. This is only a guess, but it could have happened. We will never know for sure. Why did he become a gaucho, is another thing we will never know. One thing I do know is he loved horses and was a very fine rider.

About a year after you grandfather disappeared, you grandmother and mother went to live with your grandmother's brother and sister-in-law on their ranch. That's where your mother really grew up. Anyway," continued Jeff's father, "your mother will be very happy to finally know what happened to her father. At least we know part of the story, anyway. I will try and get a call through to her as soon as we get back to the estancia." When Jeff's father had finished, Tomas and the MacLean's nodded their heads in agreement and said that is certainly what might have happened to Jeff's grandfather.

Next, Jeff led them to the little valley to get the polo ponies and to show them the claw marks left by the big cat on the floor of the shack.

·   ·   ·

When they got back to the estancia, Jeff's father was able to get a call through to Jeff's mother. When he had finished telling her the story, for the longest time, she couldn't speak. He knew she was crying and did not interrupt. When she did speak, the only words she was able to say was a thankful, "Now I know," followed by a warm, "Thank you." Before hanging up, she asked Jeff's father if he would be coming home soon. He knew she needed him and told her things had gone much smoother than expected and he could leave within the next couple of days. Jeff said he would like to stay until the auction was over and his father said that it was fine with him.

That very next day, Mr. MacLean had the estancia's blacksmith make a metal plaque and had him engrave on it the words: "This plaque is dedicated to the brave North American gaucho, who at this very sight gave his life so three friends might live."

Early on the morning Jeff's father was to leave, Jeff, his father and both MacLean's, with Tomas In the lead, rode out to the place where so many years before, the avalanche had occurred. They mounted the plaque on the side of a large, flat boulder as a tribute to the North American gaucho, and so anyone who might be passing, could see it.

Because Jeff's father had to leave sooner than expected, he did not get to go fishing this time, but he promised they would all go on their next visit.

.   .   .

After all the guests for the week's event had arrived, the atmosphere was really exciting, like a carnival or circus.

Everyone had a great time. The food was fantastic. The rodeo put on by the gauchos was a real thrill, but the polo matches were every bit as exciting as Jeff remembered. In the final match, with the neighboring estancia, Robert's team lost to them again, but this time it went into double time.

The only serious time was during the auctioning off of the polo ponies, when the bidding became fast and furious. When the sale was over, Robert told Jeff, it was the most successful they had ever had.

· · ·

At the very beginning of the week, Robert introduced Jeff to a young married couple from England. Roger, and his wife, Sue, loved to fly fish and because he was so busy, Robert asked Jeff if he would take them fishing? He told Robert he would be glad to take them. Actually, they were able to squeeze in more than one session on the river. Both Roger and Sue were accomplished fly fishers and loved it just as much as Jeff did. The three of them became fast friends and Jeff got a standing invitation to visit Roger and Sue whenever he could. They told him there was a very good trout stream running through their own property. Jeff said he would definitely come for a visit. It wasn't until later Jeff found out from Robert that Roger was a Duke and Sue a Duchess. Both were well known in England for their love of all kinds of sport.

It all passed so fast. To Jeff, it seemed the week had only begun, when it ended and the guests had all left. He really hated to see Roger and Sue leave, because they had become such close friends. It was almost time for Jeff to leave, but he and Robert were able to get in one more day of fishing on the river, and it was a good day.

· · ·

The light of day was just a sliver of silver in the eastern sky. Jeff's luggage was packed in the vehicle and it was time to leave. Robert and his father were already in the front seat waiting. He was about get in, when Tomas came out of the house. He was carrying a fairly large, flat, nearly square package. He handed the package to Jeff and said, "Here Jeff, this for you. Do not open it until you get home."

"Thank you, Tomas," Jeff said in a surprised voice, "but what is it?"

"Something to help you remember us," came Tomas' moving reply.

When Jeff got home and opened the package, it was a painting Tomas had done of the estancia. Jeff knew he would treasure it always. On the back of the paining, Tomas wrote: To our young North American friend. May he never forget us.

They were just topping the rise, where Mr. MacLean had stopped on that first day so Jeff and his father could get a good view of the estancia, when a strange thing happened. The bell in the bell tower began to ring.

"Is that the bell in your bell tower ringing?" Jeff asked.

"Yes, that's our bell," Mr. MacLean answered as he slammed on the brakes and turned off the engine, and he and Robert looked at each other with their mouths wide open in disbelief.

"Is something wrong?" asked Jeff.

"You see, Jeff, that bell only rings at very special times. It is a family tradition that has not been broken. It has never rung without the approval of the entire family. The last time it sounded was when Robert's younger sister was born. There is only one key to the door of the tower and I have it right here on my key ring," Mr. MacLean said pointing to a key.

Now, it was Jeff's mouth that dropped open. After several loud peals, the bell stopped ringing as abruptly as it had begun. The sudden quiet seemed to be almost as loud as the ringing bell. Mr. MacLean started the engine and slowly picked up speed. Nothing more was said, but the three of them knew without saying who rang the bell and they were glad.

Other books by Jack L. Parker

Tibetan Adventure